GOLD COAST ANGELS

The hottest docs, the warmest hearts, the highest drama

Gold Coast City Hospital is located right in Australia's Surfers Paradise, at the heart of the Gold Coast, just a stone's throw away from the world famous beach.
The hospital has a reputation for some of the finest doctors in their field, kind-hearted nurses and cutting-edge treatments.

With their 'work hard and play hard' motto, the staff form a warm, vibrant community where rumours, passion and drama are never far away.
Especially when there is a new arrival— fresh from Angel Mendez Hospital, NYC!

When utterly gorgeous bad-boy-with-a-heart Cade rolls into town, trouble is definitely coming to Surfers Paradise!

If you loved **NYC Angels**, you'll love the high drama and passion of this irresistible four-book Mills & Boon® Medical Romance™ series!

GOLD COAST ANGELS: TWO TINY HEARTBEATS
by Fiona McArthur

is also available this month

Dear Reader

It's autumn as I write this, and the weather's closing in on Southern Australia where I live, so right now I'm packing my togs and thongs (that's Aussie-speak for bathing costume and flip-flops) and heading for an extension to my summer. I'm flying up to the Australian Gold Coast. Why not? In Southern Queensland it's almost perennially summer, the beaches are superb, the surf's excellent—and there are lots of places that sell drinks with little umbrellas!

I'm sure the characters in Gold Coast City Hospital didn't have drinks with umbrellas in mind when they applied to work in the hospital we've set our stories in. Surely not! Our *Gold Coast Angels* are a dedicated team of young medics, whose every thought must be tuned to the medicine they live and breathe. But we've nobly allowed them some down time. We've thrown in a little surf, plus a touch of intrigue and drama, and we've definitely included romance. A *lot* of romance.

Your four dedicated Aussie authors have thus had a wonderful time playing on the Gold Coast, researching everything we needed to bring you four fantastic romances. But I've been away for too long, writing and not sun-soaking. Now there's a sun lounger with my name on it waiting up north. I can hear it calling. I can hear the surf calling. The Gold Coast's a wonderful place for lying on the sand and reading romance. Maybe I'll meet you there. I'll be the one with the umbrella.

Happy reading!

Marion Lennox

GOLD COAST ANGELS: A DOCTOR'S REDEMPTION

BY
MARION LENNOX

First published in Great Britain 2013
by Mills & Boon, an imprint of Harlequin (UK) Limited.
Harlequin (UK) Limited, Eton House, 18-24 Paradise Road,
Richmond, Surrey TW9 1SR

© Harlequin Books S.A. 2013

Special thanks and acknowledgement are given to Marion Lennox
for her contribution to the *Gold Coast Angels* series.

ISBN: 978 0 263 23379 7

Harlequin (UK) policy is to use papers that are natural, renewable
and recyclable products and made from wood grown in sustainable
forests. The logging and manufacturing process conform to the
legal environmental regulations of the country of origin.

Printed and bound in Great Britain
by CPI Antony Rowe, Chippenham, Wiltshire

Marion Lennox is a country girl, born on an Australian dairy farm. She moved on—mostly because the cows just weren't interested in her stories! Married to a 'very special doctor', Marion writes Medical Romances™, as well as Mills & Boon® Romances. (She used a different name for each category for a while—if you're looking for her past Romances search for author Trisha David as well.) She's now had well over 90 novels accepted for publication.

In her non-writing life Marion cares for kids, cats, dogs, chooks and goldfish. She travels, she fights her rampant garden (she's losing) and her house dust (she's lost). Having spun in circles for the first part of her life, she's now stepped back from her 'other' career, which was teaching statistics at her local university. Finally she's reprioritised her life, figured out what's important, and discovered the joys of deep baths, romance and chocolate. Preferably all at the same time!

GOLD COAST ANGELS

The hottest docs, the warmest hearts, the highest drama

This month, sexy lone wolf Sam is given a second chance
at life by bubbly nurse Zoe in
A DOCTOR'S REDEMPTION by Marion Lennox

And midwife Lucy's first day at work
takes an unexpected turn when gorgeous new colleague Nick
suggests she takes a pregnancy test in
TWO TINY HEARTBEATS by Fiona McArthur

Then, in November, nurse Chloe falls for brooding surgeon
and single dad Luke in
BUNDLE OF TROUBLE by Fiona Lowe

While Cade and Callie can't get that steamy one-night stand
out of their minds in
HOW TO RESIST TEMPTATION by Amy Andrews

Don't miss this fabulous four-book series full of breathtaking
drama, heartwrenching emotion and sizzling passion!

**These books are also available in eBook format
from www.millsandboon.co.uk**

CHAPTER ONE

WHY DID ACCIDENTS seem to happen in slow motion?

There seemed all the time in the world to yell a warning, to run down the beach and haul the dog out of harm's way, to get the fool driving the beach buggy to change direction, but in reality Zoe Payne had time for nothing.

She'd been sitting admiring the sunset at the spectacular surf beach five minutes' drive from Gold Coast City Hospital. A tangerine hue tinged the white crests of the breaking waves, the warm sea air filled her senses and the scene was breathtakingly lovely.

She'd also been admiring a lone surfer, far out in the waves.

He was good. Very good. The surfable waves were few and far apart, but he had all the patience in the world. He waited for just the right wave, positioned himself before the rising swell with casual ease, then rode seamlessly in before the breaking line of white water.

The scene was poetry in motion, she'd decided, and the surfer wasn't bad either. When the wave brought him close to the shore she saw him up close. He was tall, sun-bleached, ripped, and the way he surfed said he was almost a part of the sea.

But she'd also been watching a dog. The dog was lying partly concealed among the dunes, closer to the shore than the place she sat. She wouldn't have known he was there, but every time the surfer neared the shore the big brown Labrador leaped from its hiding place and surged into the shallows. The surfer came in the extra distance to greet the dog, they exchanged exuberant man-dog hugs, and then the surfer returned to the sea and the dog to its hiding place.

She'd been thinking she'd kind of like to go and talk to the dog. This was her first week at Gold Coast City and she was feeling a bit homesick, but there was something about man and dog that said these two were a team that walked alone.

Only now they weren't alone. Now a beach buggy was screaming down from the road above.

There was no way a beach buggy should be on this beach. There were signs everywhere—protected beach, no bikes, no horses, no cars.

And this wasn't a local fisherman driving quietly down for an evening's fishing. This was a hoon driver, gunning his hired beach buggy—she could see the rental signs—for all he was worth.

He hit the dunes and the buggy became almost airborne.

The dog...

She was on her feet, yelling, running, but her feet wouldn't move fast enough, her voice wouldn't yell loud enough.

Oh, dear God, no!

For the buggy had hit the dune in front of the dog and hurled right over. It crashed down, hit the next dune, was gunned to further power and roared off along the beach, leaving whatever had happened behind it.

One minute Sam Webster was paddling idly on his board, waiting for the next wave. He was about to call it a day. Surfing after dark was dumb. He knew the risks of night-feeding marine life, and risk-taking was for fools. Besides, the waves were growing fewer, and the current was taking him out. If he couldn't catch a wave soon, he was faced with a ten-minute paddle to get back to shore.

It was time to head back to the beach, take Bonnie home and head for bed.

To sleep? Possibly not. Sam Webster didn't do much sleeping any more, but hard surfing morning and night helped. His job at the hospital was high-powered and demanding. He crammed his days to the point of exhaustion, but still sleep was elusive. Nights weren't his friend.

But Bonnie needed to be home. Where was a wave when you wanted one?

And then…

He heard the beach buggy before he saw it, roaring along the beach road, and then, unbelievably, veering hard across the dunes onto the beach.

The dunes…

'Bonnie!'

He was yelling now, paddling and yelling at the same time, but the tide was turning and he wasn't making headway.

Where was a wave? *Where was a wave?*

The buggy was freewheeling along the beach.

Bonnie!

And then the buggy hit the dune where Bonnie lay.

His eyes were locked on the hollow where Bonnie had dug herself a cool spot to lie. He was willing her to emerge. Willing her to show herself.

Nothing.

A figure was running from the grassy verge above the beach. A woman. He wasn't interested. All he was interested in was Bonnie.

Where was a wave?

For one appalling moment she thought it was dead. The great, chocolate-brown Labrador was lying sprawled on the sand, a pool of blood spreading ominously fast.

She was down on her knees.

'Hey,' she said. 'Hey.' She spoke softly. The last thing she wanted was to terrify the dog even more. The eyes that looked up at her were great pools of fear, shock and pain.

But not aggression. Fear, shock and pain sometimes made even the most placid animals vicious, but Zoe knew instinctively that this dog wouldn't snap.

She was beyond it?

Maybe.

The buggy looked as if it had landed on her hind quarters. Her head, chest and front legs looked relatively unscathed, but her left hind leg… Not unscathed.

There was a gash running almost its length.

So much blood…

She hauled off her shirt, ripping it, bundling part of it into a pad and using the rest to tie the pad so she got maximum pressure, talking to the dog as she did.

'Sorry, girl, I don't want to hurt you, but I need to stop the bleeding.'

Even if she stopped it… The blood on the sand…

She had to get this dog to help. She'd seen patients go into cardiac arrest through blood loss, and this dog was losing so much...

She glanced out to sea. The surfer was frantically paddling, but he was far out and there were no waves behind him.

It'd take him maybe five minutes to reach the beach—and this dog didn't have five minutes.

She'd slowed the blood flow. She hadn't stopped it.

There was a vet's surgery near the hospital. She'd seen it the day she'd arrived, when she'd been making her first exploratory forays, searching for a supermarket. It had a sign on it, 'All Hours, Emergency'.

That's what this was, she thought as she ripped and tied her shirt. Total emergency.

Her car was right by the beach. Could she lift the dog?

She glanced again out at the surfer. He was surely the dog's owner. She should wait.

And give him a dead dog?

There was no choice. She scrawled one word in the sand. She lifted the big dog into her arms, staggering with the weight, and then, despite its weight, she found the strength to run.

It was the longest paddle of Sam's life.

The long, low waves that had been giving him such pleasure all evening had disappeared. The sea looked millpond-smooth but the tide was surging and the current was almost stronger than he could paddle against.

In a normal situation he'd let the current take him along the beach, travelling sideways to the tidal tug and gradually reaching the beach without this fight. But this wasn't a normal situation.

Bonnie.

Emily's dog.

He remembered the day Emily had brought her home. 'Look, Sammy, isn't she adorable? She was in the pet-shop window and I couldn't go past her.'

They had been medical students and dirt poor, living in a one-room university apartment. Having a dog had meant moving house, taking on more rent than they could afford and juggling impossible study hours into caring for an active dog, but Em hadn't thought of that.

She'd seen a puppy and she'd bought it. She hadn't thought of consequences.

Which was why Emily was dead, and all he had left of her was her dog, *his dog*, and his dog had disappeared, carried by a stranger up over the sand dunes to the road beyond and he couldn't see her any more and he was going out of his mind.

And finally, when he reached the beach, things weren't any better.

He dumped his board and ran, but what he found made him feel cold and sick. The hollow where Bonnie had lain was almost awash with blood.

So much blood… How could she survive blood loss like this?

Where was she?

He turned and saw three letters scrawled in the sand, rough, as if done with a foot.

'VET.'

Sensible. Dear God, sensible. But where? Where was the closest vet?

Staring at Bonnie's blood… It was so hard to think. *Think.*

There was a vet's surgery near the hospital, the one

he normally took Bonnie to. It was the closest. Surely whoever it was knew that.

He was heading up the beach, ripping his wetsuit off as he ran.

So much blood… It was impossible that she would survive.

She had to survive. Without Bonnie he had nothing left.

The veterinary hospital was open and amazingly, wonderfully, a vet came out to meet her. Maybe it was the way she'd spun into the entrance, burning rubber. Medics were clued in to hints like that, she decided, because by the time she was out of her car, a middle-aged guy wearing a clinical coat was there to help her.

'Road trauma,' she said, wasting no words, somehow shifting into medical mode. What she must look like… She'd ripped off her shirt to stop the blood flow. She was wearing a lacy bra and jeans and sandals and she was smeared with blood from the neck down—or even higher, but she wasn't looking. But the vet was looking. He took her arm and hauled her round so he could see her face on, before he even looked at the dog.

'Are you hurt?' he demanded, and she caught herself, realising he needed reassurance. Triage dictated humans before animals, even for a vet, so she needed to waste a few words.

'A buggy hit her on the beach,' she said. 'I saw it happen but, no, I'm not hurt. This is all her blood. She's not my dog—her owner's out surfing but I didn't have time to wait for him to get back in. She's bleeding out from the back leg.'

'Not now she's not,' the vet said, and he was already leaning into the car. He could see the tourniquet she'd fashioned with her shirt and he cast her a glance of approval. 'She's Bonnie,' he said, flipping the name tag on her collar. 'I know her—she's one of the local docs' dogs. Sam Webster. You're not medical yourself, are you?'

'I'm a nurse.'

'Great. I'm the only one here and I'll need help. You up for it?'

'Of course,' she said, but he hadn't waited for a response. He was already carrying the dog through the entrance to his surgery beyond.

CHAPTER TWO

He'd come to the right place. As soon as he pulled into the entrance to the veterinary surgery he could guess Bonnie had been brought here.

An ancient car was parked across the emergency entrance. It looked battered and rusty, it had obviously seen far better days, and right now the back door was swinging wide and all he could see on the back seat was blood.

There were spatters of blood on the ramp. There were spatters of blood leading to the entrance.

He felt sick.

He'd got rid of his wetsuit. He was wearing board shorts and nothing else, his feet were bare and so was his chest. He felt exposed, but the feeling was nothing to do with his lack of clothes.

Get a grip. You're a doctor, he told himself harshly. *Let's treat this as a medical emergency.*

At this time of night the vet surgery was deserted, apart from a cleaner attacking the floor with a look of disgust. He looked at Sam with even more disgust.

'Sand as well as blood. I've just cleaned this.'

'Where's my dog?'

'If you mean the half-dead Labrador the girl brought in, Doc's got her in Theatre.' He motioned to the swing doors at the end of Reception. 'Girl went in, too. You want to sit down and wait? Hey, you can't go in there. Wait…'

But Sam was gone, striding across the shiny wet floor, through the green baize doors and to what lay beyond.

He stopped as soon as the doors swung wide.

He might be an emotionally-distraught owner, he might be going out of his mind with worry, but Sam Webster was still a doctor. He was a cardiac surgeon, with additional training in paediatric cardiology. The theatres where he operated were so sterile that no bacteria would dare come within fifty feet, and he was trained enough so that barging into an operating theatre and heading straight for the dog on the table wasn't going to happen. So he stood at the door and took in the scene before him.

Bonnie was stretched out on the operating bench. There was already a drip set up in her front leg and a bag of saline hung above. The vet, Doug—he knew this guy, he was the vet who gave Bonnie his yearly shots—was filling a syringe.

There were paddles lying on the floor as if tossed aside.

Paddles.

He had it in one. Catastrophic blood loss. Heart failure.

But the vet was inserting the syringe, the girl at the head of the table was holding Bonnie's head and whispering to her and they wouldn't do that to a dead dog.

Doug glanced up and saw him. 'That'd be right,' he growled. 'Doctor arriving after the hard work's done. Isn't that right, Nurse?' He heard the tension in Doug's voice and he knew Bonnie wasn't out of the woods yet, but he also knew that this girl had got his dog here in time—or maybe not in time, but at least she stood a chance.

If she'd gone into cardiac arrest on the beach...

'How are you at anaesthetics?' Doug snapped, and he forced himself to focus on the question. Medical emergency. How many times had he had the rules drilled into him during training? Take the personal distress out of it until the crisis is over.

'I'm rusty but grounded,' he managed.

'Rusty but grounded is better than nothing. Humans, dogs, what's the difference? I'll give you the doses. I want her under and intubated and Zoe here doesn't have the skills. I've called for back-up but I can't get hold of my partner in time. You want to make yourself useful, scrub and help.'

'What's...what's the situation?' He was watching Bonnie, but he was also watching the girl—Zoe?— holding Bonnie still. They wouldn't have had time to knock her out yet, he thought. They'd have been too busy saving her life.

The girl looked...stunning. She was smeared in blood, her chestnut-brown curls were plastered across her face, she was wearing a lace bra and jeans and not much else.

She still looked stunning.

'Don't talk,' she said urgently. 'Not until you're scrubbed and can stay with her. She heard you then and she wants to get up.'

That hauled him back into medical mode. He nodded and moved to the sink, fast. He knew the last thing they needed was for Bonnie to struggle, even so much as raise her head.

'It's okay, girl, it's okay.' In the quiet he heard Zoe's

whisper. She wasn't so much holding Bonnie down as caressing her down, her face inches from Bonnie's, her hands folding the great, silky ears.

He had no doubt that this was the woman who'd saved his dog's life. He'd seen her in the distance, picking Bonnie up and carrying her up the beach. From far out in the surf he hadn't realised how slight she was. And the blood... If she'd walked into Gold Coast Central's Emergency Department looking like that she'd have the whole department pushing Code Blue.

He glanced at the floor and saw the remains of her shirt, ripped and twisted into a pad and ties. That explained why she was only wearing a bra.

She'd done this for his dog?

Was she a vet nurse? If so, how lucky was he that she'd been on the beach?

Luck? He glanced again at Bonnie and thought he needed more.

Doug was injecting the anaesthetic. Sam dried, gloved, and took over the intubation. Zoe stood aside to give him room then moved seamlessly into assistance mode.

She was obviously a vet nurse, and a good one. She was watching Doug, anticipating his needs, often preempting his curt orders. Swift, sure and competent.

Doug was good, too. He'd met this guy before and thought he was a competent vet in a family vet practice. His work now said that he was more than competent to do whatever was needed.

They worked solidly. With fluid balance restored, Bonnie's vital signs settled. Doug had all the equipment needed to do a thorough assessment and a full set of X-rays revealed more luck.

Her left hind leg was badly broken and so were a

couple of ribs, but apart from the mass of lacerations that seemed the extent of the major damage.

Her blood pressure was steadying, which meant major internal bleeding was unlikely. Amazingly, there seemed little more damage.

'I can plate that leg,' Doug said curtly. 'It's easier than trying to keep her off it for weeks. If you'll assist…'

Of course he'd assist. Sam was almost starting to hope.

He thought of the buggy crashing down on Bonnie, and he thought this outcome was either luck or a miracle. Either way he was very thankful.

And that this girl had been there as well…

She hardly spoke. She looked white-faced and shocked but her competence was never in question. Doug was a man of few words. He worked and Sam worked with him, and the white-faced girl worked as well.

They needed the full team of three. With Bonnie anaesthetised and seemingly stable, Doug decided to work on to do whatever was necessary.

'Otherwise I'll be hauling a team in to do this tomorrow,' Doug said. 'That's two doses of anaesthetic and with both of you here I don't see why I need to do that.'

Zoe wasn't asking questions. She must be desperate for a bath and a strong cup of tea with loads of sugar— or something stronger, he thought—but she didn't falter. Sam hadn't seen her before, but he had only been at the Gold Coast for a year. He'd brought Bonnie to the vet twice in that time, for routine things. Two visits were hardly enough to know the staff.

He'd like to be able to tell her to go and have a wash,

he thought, but she was needed. She'd scrubbed and gloved and was ignoring the fact that she was only in bra and jeans. She looked shocked and sick, but she was professional and capable.

And she still looked...stunning. It was the only word he could think of to describe her. A bit too thin. Huge eyes. A bit...frail?

Gorgeous.

What would she look like without the gore?

But he only had fragments of time to think about the woman beside him. Most of the time he forgot, too, that he was in board shorts and nothing else.

There was only Bonnie.

This was no simple break. Bonnie's leg would be plated for life.

Sam was no orthopaedic surgeon but he knew enough to be seriously impressed by Doug's skill. The fractured tibia was exposed and Doug took all the time he needed to remove free-floating fragments. He was encircling the remaining fragments with stainless steel, bending the plate to conform to the surface of the bone then drilling to fix bone screws. He checked and checked again, working towards maximum sta-bility, examining placement of every bone fragment to ensure as much natural healing—bone melding to bone—as he could. Finally he started the long process of suturing the leg closed.

Which was just as well, Sam thought. Zoe looked close to the edge.

Bu they still needed her. She was doing the job of two nurses, assisting, preparing equipment, anticipat-ing every need.

Bonnie was so lucky with her rescue team. The big

dog lay under their hands and he thought he couldn't have asked for a more highly-skilled partnership.

He owed this girl so much. If there was back-up he'd stand her down now, but there was no one. She'd already done more than he could ever expect—and he was asking more.

But finally they were done. Doug stepped back from the table and wiped a sleeve over his forehead.

'I reckon she'll make it,' he said softly, and as he said it Sam saw Zoe's eyes close.

She was indeed done. She swayed and he moved instinctively to grab her—this wouldn't be the first time a nurse or doctor passed out after coping with a tense and bloody procedure. But then she had control of herself again, and was shaking him off and moving aside so Doug could remove the breathing tube.

'I… That's great,' she whispered. 'If it's okay with you, I might leave you to it.'

'Yeah, you look like a bomb site,' Doug said bluntly. 'Take her home, Sam, and then come back. Bonnie'll take a while to wake. I won't leave her and you can be back before she needs reassuring.'

'I have my car…' Zoe said.

'I've seen your car and I'm looking at you,' Doug said drily. 'You drive through town looking like that you'll have the entire Gold Coast police force thinking there's been an axe murder. Leave the keys here. I'll park it round the back and you can fetch it tomorrow. Where do you live?'

'The hospital apartments,' she said. 'They're only two blocks away. I can drive.'

'You tell me those legs aren't shaking,' Doug retorted. 'You've done a magnificent job, lass, but now you need help yourself. You have some great staff,

Sam. You were damned lucky to have your colleague on the beach.'

'My colleague...?'

'You realise Bonnie arrested?' Doug went on. 'Heart stopped twice. With blood loss like that it's a wonder she made it. A miracle more like. If Zoe hadn't got her here... Well, if she cops a speeding fine for her trip here, I'm thinking you ought to pay it.'

'I'd pay for more,' Sam said, stunned—and confused. 'You're not a vet nurse?'

'I'm a nurse at Gold Coast City,' she managed. 'I'd rather go home by myself.'

A nurse. A human nurse. One of his *colleagues*?

'Take her home, Sam,' Doug told him. 'Now. Take a gown from the back room, Zoe, so you look less like a bomb victim, but go home now. You deserve a medal and if Sam doesn't give you one I'll give you one myself. Go.'

'I'll be giving her a medal,' Sam growled. 'I'll give her a truckload if she'll take it. What you've done...'

'It's okay,' Zoe managed. 'Enough with the medals. Doug's right, I just need to go home.'

She wanted to go home but she didn't want this man to take her.

She wanted, more than anything, to slide behind the wheel of her car, drive back to Gold Coast Central, sneak in the back way and find a bath and bed.

But there was no 'back way', no way to get back into the hospital without attracting attention, and Doug was right, she and her car were a mess.

Sam was taking her home?

He ushered her outside where his Jeep was parked next to her car and she thought...she thought...

This guy was a doctor? A colleague?

He was still only wearing board shorts. Unlike her, though, he didn't look gruesome. He looked like something from the cover of one of the myriad surfing magazines in the local shops.

The Gold Coast was surfing territory, and many surfers here lived for the waves. That's what this guy looked like. He was bronzed, lean, ripped, his brown hair bleached blond by sun and sea, his green eyes crinkled and creased from years of waiting for the perfect wave.

He was a doctor and a surfer.

Where did dog owner come into that?

He grabbed a T-shirt from the back seat of his Jeep and hauled it on. He looked almost normal, she thought, even after what had happened. His dog was fixed and he was ready to move on.

She glanced down at her oversized theatre gown and the bloodied jeans beneath them and something just...cracked.

For hours now she'd been clenching her emotions down while she'd got the job done. She looked at the mess that was her car, her independence, her freedom, she looked down at her disgusting jeans—and control finally broke.

'Let's go,' he said, but she shook her head.

'What were you thinking?' she managed, trying hard to keep her voice low, calm, incisive, clear. 'Leaving her waiting on the beach? Leaving her alone? To be so far out and leave her there... If I hadn't been there she'd be dead. You have a dog like Bonnie and you just desert her. Of all the stupid, crass, negligent, cruel...

'Do you know how lucky you are to have a dog? Of course you don't. You're a doctor, you're a healthy, fit, surfer boy. You can buy any dog you want, so you just buy her and then you don't care that she loves you, so she lies there and waits and waits. I was watching her—and she adores you, and you abandoned her and it nearly killed her. If I hadn't been there it would have! She nearly died because you didn't care!'

So much for calm, incisive and clear. She was yelling at the top of her lungs, and he was standing there watching, just watching, and she wanted to hit him and she thought for one crazy moment that it'd be justifiable homicide and she could hear the judge say, 'He deserved everything that was coming to him.'

Only, of course, she couldn't hit him. Somehow she had to get herself under control. She hiccuped on a sob and that made her angrier still because she didn't cry, she never cried, and she knew she was being irrational, it was just…it was just…

The last few days had been crazy. She'd spent her whole life in one small community, closeted, cared for. The move here from Adelaide might seem small to some, but for Zoe it was the breaking of chains that had been with her since childhood.

It was the right thing to do, to move on, but, still, the new job, the new workplace, the constant calls from her parents—and from Dean, who still couldn't understand why she'd left—were undermining her determination and making her feel bleak with homesickness.

But she would not give in to Dean. 'You'll come to your senses, Zoe, I know you will. Have your fling but come home soon. All we want to do is look after you.'

Aaagh!

She did not want to go home. She did not want to be looked after.

But neither did she want to yell at this stranger or

stand in a theatre gown covering a bra and jeans, looking disgusting and feeling tears well in her eyes and
rage overwhelm her, and know that somehow she had
to get back into the hospital apartments, past strang-
ers. Plus she'd intended to buy milk on the way home
and…and…

And she would do this.

She fumbled under her gown to fetch her car keys.
She had to lift the thing but what the heck, this guy
had seen her at her worst anyway. She grabbed her car
keys from her jeans pocket but Sam lifted them from
her hand before she could take a step towards the car.

'We go in my car,' he said in a voice that said he
was talking her down, doctor approaching lunatic, and
she took a step back at that.

'I'm not crazy. I might have yelled too much but
you deserve it.'

'You think I don't know it? I love Bonnie,' he said.
'I deserve everything you throw at me and more,
apart from the accusation that I could just buy another dog because I never could. I am deeply, deeply
sorry for what happened. The fact that Bonnie has
been watching me surf since she was a pup twelve
years ago doesn't mean it's okay now. The fact that
it's a secluded beach and the guys in the buggy were
there illegally doesn't mean it's okay either. Years ago
Bonnie would have watched the whole beach. Tonight
she just watched me and she paid the price. Zoe, you're
upset and you have every right to be but I can't let you
go home alone.'

'You can't stop me. It's my car. Get out of the way.'

'Zoe, be sensible. Get in the car, there's a good
girl…'

He sounded just like Dean—and she smacked him.

* * *

She'd never smacked a man in her life.

She'd never smacked anyone in her life. Or anything. Even in the worst of the bleak days, when the first transplant had failed, when she'd heard the doctors telling her parents to prepare for the worst, she'd hung in there, she'd stayed in control, she hadn't cried, she hadn't kicked the wall, she hadn't lashed out at anything.

Not because she hadn't wanted to but it had always seemed that if she did, if she let go of her relentless control, she'd never get it back. She'd drop into a black and terrifying chasm. She was far better gripping her nails into her palms until they bled and smiling at her parents and pretending she hadn't heard, that things were normal, that life was fine.

And here, now, the first week of her new life, standing in the dusk in a veterinary surgeon's car park, with a doctor from the hospital where she wanted to start her new life…

She'd hit him.

The chasm was there, and she was falling.

She stared at him in horror. The yelling had stopped. There was nothing left in her and she couldn't say a word.

His face stung where her hand had swiped him in an open-palmed slap. The sound of the slap seemed to echo in the still night.

She was staring at him like the hounds of hell were after her.

It didn't take a genius to know this woman didn't normally slap people. Neither did it take a genius to know she was on some sort of precipice. She was teetering on the edge of hysteria. She was hauling herself back, but she was terrified she wasn't going to make it.

What did you do with a woman who'd just slapped you? Walk away, reacting as he'd been taught all his life to react to people who were out of control?

Her eyes were huge in her white face. She was dressed in an oversized theatre gown and blood-splattered jeans and she looked like something out of a war zone.

And he could tell that there were things in this woman's life that lay behind even the appalling events of the last few hours.

She'd hit him and she was looking at him as if she'd shot him. In his private life he avoided emotional contact like the plague. But with this woman... What was it about her?

Walk away? No.

He took her hands in his and he tugged her forward. He folded her into his arms and held her, as he'd not held a woman for years.

She'd slapped him.

He didn't care. He just...held.

One minute she was out-of-control crazy. The next minute she was being hugged.

She was rigid with shock, but maybe rigid was too mild a word for it. She felt like she was frozen.

If she moved... But there was no if. She *couldn't* move. She didn't know who she would be if she moved. She would be some out-of-control creature who screamed and hit...

She had to apologise. She had to pull away and say she was sorry, but her body wouldn't obey. Tremors were starting, shudders that ran all through her. If she pulled away she'd have nothing to hold her. All she could do was let this man—this stranger—keep her close and stop her crumpling.

She was falling into him and he was holding her as she had to be held. She was moulding to him, feeling the warmth and strength of him, feeling the steadiness of his heartbeat, and it was as if in some way he was giving hers back.

She was delusional. Crazy. She needed to pull herself together, but not yet, not yet. For now she could only stand within his arms while the world somehow righted itself, restored itself to order, until she finally found the strength to pull away and face the consequences of what she'd done.

Sam specialised in paediatric cardiology. He treated children and babies with heart problems. In his working life he faced parents on the edge of control—or who had tipped over into an abyss of grief. He never got used to it. He'd learned techniques to keep control of his emotions. To express quiet sympathy, to offer hope when hope was possible, to listen when listening was all he had to give.

But he'd never felt like he did now.

This made no sense. Yes, his dog was hurt. Yes, it had been an appalling evening but if this woman was a trained nurse… For her to collapse like this…

For him to feel like this…

Why? What was it with this woman that was making his heart twist?

He held her and felt her take strength from him. He felt the rigidity ease, felt her slump against him, and he felt her quietly gather herself.

He should move her away but his rigid protection

of personal space wasn't working right now. She was so vulnerable…and yet what she'd done, how she'd acted, had taken pure strength. There was no way he could let her down now, and when finally she found the strength to tug away he was aware of a sharp stab of loss.

She hadn't cried. She was still white-faced, but she was dry-eyed and drained.

She shoved her hands through her curls, tucking stray wisps behind her ears, and he felt an almost irresistible urge to help her. To fix a tiny curl that had escaped.

He wasn't an idiot. He'd been slapped once. It behoved a man to stay still and silent, and wait for her to make the first move.

'I…I'm sorry,' she managed at last.

'It's okay,' he told her, striving hard to lighten what was an unbelievably heavy situation. 'I was feeling guilty about Bonnie. Now I can feel virtuously aggrieved at being assaulted.'

'And I get the guilt instead?'

'Exactly,' he said, and tried a smile.

She didn't smile back. She looked up at him, and he thought, whatever had gone before, this woman wasn't one to crumple. There was strength there. Real strength.

'Hitting's never okay,' she said.

'You were swatting flies,' he said. 'And missed.'

She did smile then. It was the merest glimmer but it was still a smile and it made him feel…

Actually, he didn't know how it made him feel. Holding her, watching her…

Why was this woman touching him? Why did he look at her and want to know more?

It was Bonnie, he told himself. It was the emotions of almost losing his dog. That's all it was.

'Let me take you home,' he said carefully, and took a step back, as if she might swipe him again.

The smile appeared again, rueful but there.

'I'm safe,' she told him. 'Unarmed.' She tucked her arms carefully behind her back and he grinned.

'Excellent. Would you accept my very kind offer of a ride home?'

'I'll stain the Jeep.'

'I'm a surfer. I have a ton of towels.'

'I need milk,' she said.

And he thought excellent—practicalities, minutiae were the way to get back on an even keel.

'Because?'

'Because I've run out,' she said. She took a deep breath, steadying herself as she spoke, and he knew she knew minutiae were important.

She'd been in the abyss, too? There seemed such a core recognition, at a level he didn't recognise, that it was an almost physical link.

But she seemed oblivious to it. 'I'm on duty at six tomorrow morning,' she said. 'I have no milk. How can I have coffee with no milk? And how can I start work with no coffee?'

'I see your need,' he said gravely. 'And I'm trained for triage. Priority one, the lady needs milk. Priority two, the lady needs home, wash, sleep. I can cope with milk and home. Can you take it from there?'

It was the right thing to say. Setting limits. Giving her a plan. He'd used this with parents of his patients hovering at the edges of control, and it worked now.

There were no more arguments. She gave him another smile, albeit a weak one, and he led her to his car.

He climbed in beside her, but still he felt strange. Why?

Forget imagined links, he told himself. This was crazy. He didn't do emotional connection. He would not.

Get this night over with, he told himself. Buy the lady some milk and say goodnight.

He drove a great vehicle for surfing. It was no doctor's car, she thought as he threw a heap of towels on the front seat. The Jeep was battered, coated with sand and salt, and liberally sprinkled with Labrador hair. Any qualms she had about spoiling the beauty of one of the sleek, expensive sets of wheels she was used to seeing in most doctors' car parks went right out the window.

Sam wasn't your normal doctor.

He didn't look your normal doctor either. He was sand- and salt-stained as well, with his sun-bleached hair and crinkled eyes telling her that surfing was something he did all the time, as much a part of him as his medicine must be.

But he was a doctor, and a good one, she suspected. She'd seen his skill at stitching. She'd also heard the transition from personal to professional as he'd coped with her emotional outburst.

Though there'd been personal in there as well. There'd been raw emotion as he'd seen Bonnie—and there'd been something more than professional care as he'd held her.

Well, she'd saved his dog.

She was trying to get a handle on it. She was trying to fit the evening's events into the impersonal. Nurse saves doctor's dog, nurse angry at doctor for leaving dog on beach, nurse hits doctor, doctor hugs nurse.

It didn't quite fit.

'I'm normally quite sane,' she ventured as he pulled up outside a convenience store.

'Me, too.' He grinned. 'Mostly. What sort of milk?'

'White.'

His grin widened. 'What, no unpasteurised, low-fat, high-calcium, no permeate added…'

'Oi,' she said. 'White.'

He chuckled and went to buy it. She watched him go, lean, lithe, tanned, muscled legs, board shorts, T-shirt, salt-stiff hair—everything about him screaming surfer.

He was pin-up material, she thought suddenly. He was the type of guy whose picture she'd have pinned on her wall when she'd been fifteen.

She'd pinned these sorts of pictures all over her wall when she'd been a kid. Her parents had had a board they'd brought in to her various hospital wards to make her feel at home. She'd had pictures of surfing all over it. She would lie and watch the images of lean bodies catching perfect waves and dream…

But then Sam was back with her milk and she had to haul herself back to the here and now.

'My purse is in my car,' she said, suddenly horrified.

'I'll fix it,' he said. 'You'll get it back tonight.'

She knew he would. *I'll fix it.*

She actually didn't like it all that much. Other people fixing stuff for her…

She had to get a grip here. Getting her purse and paying for her milk were not enough to start a war over.

She subsided while he drove the short distance to

the hospital apartment car park. The parking space he drove into indicated it belonged to 'Mr Sam Webster. Paediatric Cardiology'.

Mr. That meant he was a surgeon.

Paediatric cardiology. Clever.

She glanced across at him and tried to meld the two images together—the specialist surgeons she'd worked with before and the surfer guy beside her.

'I clean up okay,' he said, and it felt weird that he'd guessed her thoughts. 'I make it a rule never to wear board shorts when consulting. Hey, Callie!'

A woman was pulling in beside them—Dr Callie Richards, neonatal specialist. Zoe had met this woman during the week and was already seriously impressed. Callie was maybe five years older than Zoe but a world apart in medical experience. In life experience, too, Zoe had thought. She'd seemed smart, confident, kind—the sort of colleague you didn't want to meet when you were looking…like she was looking now. She'd also seemed aloof.

But Sam was greeting her warmly, calling her over.

'Callie, could you spare us a few minutes?' he called. 'We've had a bit of a traumatic time. Bonnie was hit by a car.'

'Bonnie!' Callie's face stilled in shock and Zoe realised she knew the dog. Maybe the whole hospital knew Bonnie, she decided, thinking back to those trusting Labrador eyes. Bonnie was the sort of dog who made friends.

'We think she'll be okay,' Sam said hurriedly, responding to the shock on Callie's face, 'but I need to get back to the vet's. This is Zoe…' He looked a query at Zoe. 'Zoe…'

'Payne,' Zoe said. She was on the opposite side of

the Jeep from Sam and Callie, and knowing how she looked she was reluctant to move.

'I know Zoe,' Callie said, smiling at her. 'New this week? From Adelaide?'

That was impressive. One brief meeting in the wards, doctor and nurse, and Callie had it.

'Yeah, well, she's had a baptism by fire,' Sam said grimly. 'I was out in the surf when Bonnie was hit, and she saved her life. We've just spent two hours operating and Zoe rocks. But now she's covered in gore and she's got a bit of delayed shock. I don't want to leave her but I need—'

'To get back to Bonnie—of course you do.' And Callie moved into caretaker mode, just like that. 'Go, Sam, I'll take care of Zoe.'

'I don't need—'

'Let Sam go and then we'll discuss it,' Callie said, and Zoe hauled herself together—again—and gave a rueful smile. Sam handed Callie Zoe's milk, as Zoe climbed out of the Jeep. Then, he was gone.

Callie was brisk, efficient and not about to listen to quibbles. She ushered Zoe into the lift and when it stopped on the first floor to admit a couple of nurses she held up her hand to stop them coming in.

'Closed for cleaning,' she said, and grinned and motioned to Zoe. 'Or it should be. Catch the next lift, ladies.'

The lift closed smoothly and they were alone again.

When they reached the apartment Zoe realised her keys were in her purse. No problem—one phone call and Callie had the caretaker there, and he didn't ask questions either. There was something about Callie that precluded questions.

Or argument. Zoe gave up, let herself be steered into the bathroom, stood for ten minutes under a steaming shower and emerged in her bathrobe, gloriously clean. Two plates of toast and eggs were on her kitchen counter with two steaming mugs of tea, and Callie was sitting over them looking as if this was completely normal, like they were flatmates and it was Callie's turn to cook.

'I hope you don't mind,' she said. 'But I'm starving, and there's nothing in my apartment. I was going to ring for pizza but you have enough to share.'

Zoe smiled and slid into a chair and thought she should protest but she was all protested out.

And the toast smelled great. She hadn't realised she was hungry. They ate in what seemed companionable silence. Zoe cradled her tea, her world righted itself somehow and when finally Callie asked questions she was ready to answer.

'How's Bonnie?' she asked first, and Zoe thought she was right in her surmise that Bonnie was a beloved presence in this hospital.

'She has a fractured leg, now plated. Lots of lacerations and two broken ribs, but Doug—the vet—seems confident that she'll be okay.'

'Thank God for that,' Callie said. 'Half the hospital would break its collective heart if she died—not to mention our Sam. Those two are inseparable.'

'He left her on the beach,' Zoe said carefully, trying not to sound judgemental, 'while he surfed. She was hit by a dune buggy.'

Callie closed her eyes. 'Damn. But that beach is closed to anything but foot traffic.'

'You know where we were?'

'Sam always surfs at the Spit at the Seaway. The

surf's great, dogs are permitted off leash and it's the safest place for Bonnie.'

'He still shouldn't have left her,' Zoe said stubbornly, and Callie shrugged and started making more tea.

'Okay, I'll give you some back story,' she said. 'You need to get used to this hospital, by the way. Everyone knows everything about everybody. If you want things kept private, forget it. I don't normally add to it, but tonight you've earned it. Bonnie was Sam's fiancée's dog. According to reports, Emily was wild, passionate and more than a little foolhardy. She surfed every night—they both did. With Bonnie. When Emily bought her as a pup Sam tried to talk her into exercising her and then leaving her in the car while they surfed, but Bonnie was Emily's dog and Emily simply refused.

'So now Bonnie's in her declining years but what she loves most in the world is lying on the beach at dusk, waiting for Sam to come in. If Sam leaves her at home, or in the Jeep, she'll howl until the world thinks she's being massacred. For months she howled because she missed Emily and Sam decided he couldn't take her beach away from her as well.'

'So...what happened to Emily?' Zoe asked.

'Killed by carelessness,' Callie retorted. 'Not that Sam will admit it, but there it is. They went down to the beach to surf but the waves were dumpers, crashing too close to shore. Sam knew it, they both knew it, but Emily went out anyway. Word is that she simply did what she wanted. She was clever and bright and she twisted the world round her finger.

'That night she and Sam had words. Sam took Bonnie for a walk along the beach to let off steam and

Emily took her board out, got dumped and broke her neck. To this day Sam thinks he should have picked her up and carted her off the beach by force, but I guess it's like telling Bonnie she can't stay on the beach on her own. Immoveable object means unimaginable force. One of them has to give.'

'Oh,' Zoe said in a small voice, and Callie gave her a swift, appraising glance.

'Let me guess—you gave Sam a lecture?'

'I…might have.'

'And that red mark on his face? The mark that looks suspiciously like finger marks?'

'Oh…' She felt herself blush from the toes up.

'It'll settle,' Callie said, grinning widely. 'They don't usually bruise with the fingermarks still show-ing. And I promise I won't tell.'

'How do you know…about the fingermarks?' Zoe managed, and Callie's smile died. There was a mo-ment's awkward pause and then Callie seemed to re-lent. She shrugged.

'I worked in a women's refuge for a while,' she said curtly in a voice that told Zoe not to go there. 'I was getting over a mistake myself. But I wouldn't worry. You saved Sam's dog, and I suspect even if the world knew you'd hit him he'd consider it a small price. Do you want to sleep in tomorrow? I can alter your shifts.'

She was changing the subject, Zoe thought, steer-ing away from the personal, and she thought there were things behind this woman's competent facade…

As there were things behind Sam's surfer image.

She should think about sleeping in. She tried for a whole two seconds, but the warmth, the food, the ef-fects of the evening's fright suddenly coalesced into one vast fog of weariness. It was like the blinds were coming down whether she willed them or not.

'I'll be fine for tomorrow,' she managed. 'But I do need to sleep.'

'I'll tuck you in,' Callie said cheerfully. 'Bedroom. Come.'

'I don't need tucking in,' she said, affronted.

'Remind me to ask when I want to know what you need,' Callie retorted. 'I'm thinking Sam Webster is going to ring me from the vet's to find out how you are and I'm telling him I've tucked you into bed, whether you wanted it or not.'

By midnight Doug was sufficiently happy with Bonnie to order Sam home.

'I'll be checking on her hourly. I'll sleep when I'm relieved in the morning but I suspect you have work tomorrow. Right? So, home. Bed.'

Bonnie was sleeping soundly, heavily sedated. Sam fondled her soft ears but she didn't respond, too busy sleeping.

Doug was right.

He headed out to the car park. Doug had locked Zoe's car but it still blocked the entrance.

He needed to retrieve her purse, and he might as well move it before handing the keys back to Doug.

It took him three minutes to get it started and Doug came out to help. They shifted it and then stood looking at it in disgust, not only because it was blood-soaked.

'She's driven that thing from Adelaide,' Sam said at last. 'How?'

'Blind faith,' Doug said. 'Some wrecking yard must have paid her to cart it away.'

It was structurally sound, Sam thought, but only just. Once upon a time it had been a little blue sedan, but its original panels had been replaced with whatever anyone could find. Some were painted bright orange with anti-rust. Some looked like they'd been attacked by a sledgehammer.

When running, the car sounded like a wheezing camel. Even the drive from entrance to car park was bumpy.

'There's a roadworthy sticker on the front,' Doug said. 'You reckon that's because she needs to prove it to the cops half a dozen times a day?' He grinned. 'Never mind, it did its job. It got your dog here in time. Girl and car both need a medal.'

'Yeah,' Sam said absently. 'I need to fix this.'

He bade Doug goodnight and headed back to his Jeep. It was a grubby surfer truck but compared to Zoe's it was luxurious.

He should go back to the hospital. Friday was a normal working day. In eight hours he'd be on the wards.

Zoe would be there in six.

Zoe…

His head was doing strange things.

He climbed into his truck and headed where he always headed when he needed to clear his mind.

The beach was deserted. A full moon hung in a cloudless sky. His board lay where he'd dumped it hours ago. Just as well the tide had been going out, he thought, but, then, he'd been granted a miracle and a surfboard would have been a small price to pay for Bonnie's life.

He needed to pay…something.

The hoons in the beach buggy would pay. Zoe had got a clear view of them, the hire-car logo, even part of the number plate. Doug had already made a call to the cops.

But Zoe?

What was it about her that twisted something inside him?

'Maybe the fact that she saved your dog?' he said drily, out loud. 'Maybe that'd make anyone seem special.'

But there was something about her...

A heroic run with a dog far too big for her. An anger that he'd deserved.

But more. What?

Where were his thoughts taking him?

He was trying hard to haul them back on track. Sam Webster was a man who walked alone. He'd had one disastrous relationship. He'd loved Emily, but he hadn't been able to protect her from herself. She'd died because of it, leaving him gutted and guilty and alone.

That night replayed in his head, over and over. Emily had had a stressful day in the wards and had come home to a letter saying she'd missed a promotion. Her mood had been foul as they'd headed to the beach. There'd been a storm and the surf had been unpredictable. He'd suggested a close-to-shore swim instead of their usual surf, but Emily had been coldly determined.

'The surf's fine. Sure, it's dumping but we're experienced enough to know which waves to leave alone. I've had enough people telling me what I can't do today. Surf with me, Sam, or leave me be.'

He let her be. He was fed up. In truth he'd been growing more and more fed up with Emily's erratic mood swings and her insistence that everything be done her way. He watched Emily for a while but she'd gone far out, waiting for the perfect wave, so he and Bonnie headed along the beach to walk out their wait.

They turned just as Emily lost patience and caught a wave she must have known was dangerous.

He remembered yelling. He remembered seeing Emily rise, catching the beginning of the curving swell, and he remembered seeing her look towards the beach, towards him. She waved and her wave was almost triumphant.

And then the wave sucked her high, curled and tossed her onto the sandbank with a force that even today made him shudder.

Enough. Don't think about it. That had been five years ago. Surely the memory should have faded by now. And what was he doing, thinking of it tonight?

Because he'd met Zoe?

This was crazy. Where his thoughts were taking him was just plain weird. She was just another woman and there were plenty of women in his life. Half his colleagues were female. He had his mother, his sisters, his workmates, and for years their position in his life had been carefully compartmentalised.

Zoe…the way he was feeling…it didn't fit.

Maybe it was because he owed her, he decided. He did owe her, big time, and Sam Webster always paid his debts.

Her car was a wreck.

Excellent. His mind cleared. He had a way to pay his debt and move on.

And he needed to move on, because for some reason it felt really important that he stop thinking about Zoe Payne. He needed to pay the debt and get her out of his mind.

CHAPTER THREE

ZOE SLEPT FITFULLY, waking during the night to flash-backs—to dune buggies crashing down, to Sam's haunted face, to the thoughts of the mess in her car. She slept enough to function, however. Uniformed and professional, she hit the wards with determined cheer—and found she was a minor celebrity.

She'd been at Gold Coast City for almost a week. Her new colleagues had been friendly enough but she still felt very much an outsider. This morning, though, Ros, the ward clerk, met her with a beaming smile and practically boomed her welcome.

'Here she is, our Zoe the lifesaver. You've saved our Bonnie!'

'*Our* Bonnie?' she said faintly.

'Everyone in the hospital loves Bonnie,' Ros told her. 'When she's not surfing with Sam, she comes in as a companion dog. We use her for the oldies or for distressed kids. If Sam tells her to stay with a needy patient she treats them as her new best friend until Sam comes to pick her up again. I can't tell you how many patients she's calmed and comforted. And the hoons nearly killed her.'

Her face lost its beam and creased in distress. 'Of all the…well, never mind, we heard the cops have already charged them. The report from the vet half an hour ago said Bonnie's on the mend, and Sam says to tell you he left your purse downstairs in the safe in Admin for you to collect when you go off duty. How lucky was it that you were there? Callie says you saved her.'

'I was glad to help,' Zoe muttered, embarrassed, and headed to changeover fast, only to be met with more congratulations and thanks.

It went on all day. She was tired, she was still feeling fragile, but by the time her shift ended she seemed to be best friends with everyone in the hospital.

At three she was done. Yay, Friday. The weekend stretched before her, and even fatigue didn't stop it seeming endless with possibilities. Her first weekend here. Her first time alone.

It felt fantastic.

She walked down to Admin to collect her purse, and hummed as she hit the lifts. Last night had been horrible, but the outcome looked good. This job seemed great. She'd been rostered onto the paediatric ward for older kids. She'd been run off her feet all day—which she loved—and somehow what had happened last night seemed to have made her accepted as a part of the Gold Coast team faster than she'd thought possible.

She had an almost irresistible urge to ring Dean and gloat.

How childish was that? She grinned, the doors of the lift opened at the administration floor—and Sam Webster was waiting for her.

Sort of.

This was a different Sam Webster.

Last night he'd looked every inch a surfer. Now he looked every inch a cardiologist.

He must have been consulting rather than operating, she thought, dazed. He was wearing the most beautiful suit—Italian, she thought, and then wondered wryly what she would know about Italian suits. But the sleek, blue, pinstriped suit looked like it was moulded to him. His shirt was crisp, white, expensive-looking, and the only hint that he worked with kids was the elephants embroidered on his blue silk tie.

This was an image that would give frantic parents reassurance that they were in the hands of the best.

He looked the best.

Why was she standing here, gawking, when she should be doing, saying...something?

She managed a smile and moved forward, squashing the dumb, irrational wish that she wasn't in her nursing pants and baggy top, that her hair was free and not hauled into a practical work knot, that she had some decent make-up on—and she didn't look like she'd just come off a long, hard shift.

'Hi,' she managed. 'They tell me Bonnie's still good. Actually, everyone tells me Bonnie's still good. I hadn't realised she was a celebrity.'

'She has good friends,' he said, smiling at her in such a way that her heart did a crazy twist. 'She made a new very good friend last night. Callie told me your shift finished at three. I came down to make sure you got your purse.'

'I'm getting it now,' she said, uselessly, and then couldn't think of anything else to say.

He had a faint mark on his cheek. Callie was right, the fingermarks had faded, but the bruise was still there. It made her want to crawl under the floor and stay there.

'It doesn't hurt,' he said, and grinned, and she flushed. How did he know what she was thinking?

'I'm sorry.'

'Sorry that it doesn't hurt?'

'Of course not.' Her chin tilted a bit and she regained her bearings. If he was going to tease...

'I've fixed your car,' he told her, and his grin faded but the faint, teasing mischief was still behind his eyes. 'Come and see.'

'It's not at the vet's?'

'The least I could do was bring it back here. Grab your purse and I'll show you where.' Then, as she still hesitated—what was it with this man that had her disconcerted?—he smiled at the girl at the desk, who handed over her purse, having obviously been listening to every word of their conversation, and he ushered her out to the car park.

That made her feel even more disconcerted. He was so...*gorgeous*. She was in her nurse's uniform.

People were glancing at them, smiling at Sam, smiling at her as if she was somehow attached to Sam. It felt weird.

'You didn't have to fix my car,' she told him as he led her across the car park. 'How did you get it done so fast?'

'What do you do when you're faced with a laundry basket full of dirty shirts and you need a clean shirt straight away?' he asked.

'I...' Uh-oh. What she suddenly suspected was dumb—wasn't it? Surely.

'You buy a new one,' he told her, confirming her lunatic thought in five words. 'Or, in your case, a good second-hand one because I thought a brand-new one might be a bit over the top.' And he stopped and motioned to a small white sedan parked right next to where they were standing. It was the same model as hers, only about twenty years younger. It was about a hundred years less battered.

'It's two years old,' he told her, 'but it's a take-a-little-old-lady-to-church-on-Sunday vehicle. The local dealer had a son born with a mitral valve disorder. I'm still running routine checks on Dan's son after successful surgery, but he's doing brilliantly, and Dan's assured me this vehicle is almost as good as his kid's heart.'

'You bought me a car?'

'I need to thank you,' he said gently. 'You saved my dog's life. Doug and I could barely get your car started last night and we thought it'd cost more to clean than you'd get for it if you sold it. I'm a surgeon and a well-qualified one at that. I'm not married. I have no kids. All I have is my dog. Thanks to your actions last night I still have her. I can easily afford to do this, and I hope you'll accept with pleasure.'

She stared at the car. It was little and white and clean. It looked a very nice car. It looked very dependable.

It looked sensible.

She thought back to the bucket of bolts she'd driven from Adelaide. She thought of all the times she'd had to stop.

She'd bought a mechanic's manual in Adelaide before she'd left and she'd studied it with one of her sisters' boyfriends. She'd spent half the time she'd taken to get here sitting on the roadside studying that book or ringing her sister's boyfriend and having him talk her through what she needed to do.

She looked again at the little white car.

I hope you'll accept with pleasure.

Why not? She had no doubt this guy could afford to buy her a car. It'd be years before she could afford one this good—and she *had* saved his dog.

'But it's not my car,' she heard herself say, before the sensible side of her could do any more sensible thinking.

'This is better.' He was eyeing her sideways, like she was a sandwich short of a picnic.

'Yes,' she said. 'It's lovely. I dare say there's some other little old lady who'll love driving it to church on Sundays.' She took a deep breath. 'But not me. It's a great offer, but it's way out of bounds of what's reasonable. I don't want to be indebted—'

'Neither do I,' he said flatly.

'You shouldn't feel indebted. I saved your dog for your dog, not for you. Besides, this is ridiculous. Pay for cleaning, yes, but a new car?'

'It's not a new car.'

'Okay, it's not, but I'm still not accepting it. And, yes, I know you can afford it but I'd still feel indebted.'

She took a deep breath, seeing that he really wanted her to accept it, knowing that, yes, to this man on consultant's wages this car was a small thing, knowing that also for some reason indebtedness was almost as big a deal for him as it was for her. But for him to hand his obligation over to her...

She thought of the indescribable pleasure she'd felt when she'd slipped behind the wheel of her battered little vehicle and she thought that feeling was far too important to let go. There was no way she was giving that feeling up just to make this man feel better.

'I love my little car,' she said.

'That's crazy. It's a bomb.'

She'd slapped him once. She wouldn't slap him again, even though her slapping fingers itched. Besides, she conceded, he was right. It was a bomb—but it was *her* bomb.

He'd gone to a lot of trouble to buy this car for her, she conceded. Anger was inappropriate. He deserved an explanation, even though she didn't much want to give it.

'I haven't had very much money,' she told him. 'Nor...nor have I had much independence. My car is the first big thing I've ever owned. For me. I know it's a wreck but I bought it with my eyes wide-open.

'My sister's dating a mechanic. Susy spent her summer sunbaking on our back lawn while Tony mooned over her, so I persuaded him to teach me about cars while he mooned. I've learned a whole lot about the insides of cars. I have a great car manual. I have excellent tools and it gives me huge pride to keep her running.' Another deep breath. 'You don't know how much pride.'

'Is this because of the kidney transplant?' he asked, and her world stood still.

Kidney transplant.

The words hung.

He knew, she thought, stunned beyond belief. No one here was supposed to know.

A new life. That's what this was supposed to be. From the time she was eight years old, when she'd first come home from school feeling dreadful, Zoe Payne had been categorised as a renal patient. That's how she'd been treated. As an invalid. She'd been cosseted by her parents and her siblings, by her teachers and doctors and nurses and the kids around her.

Her kidneys had finally failed completely. There'd been the agonising wait and then a transplant that had failed as well.

That was when her parents had thought she was going to die.

The wait then had been interminable. She'd held on by a thread while her two sisters and her brother had grown through adolescence into adulthood, while the kids she'd met in the brief times she'd gone to school had lived normal lives, taken risks, got colds that hadn't landed them in hospital, hadn't been co-cooned with worry and with care.

And then, finally, miraculously, she'd had a transplant that worked.

'You have your whole life ahead of you now,' her renal surgeon had told her at her last check-up. 'Career, babies, the world's there for you to do what you'd like with. Go for it.'

Only, of course, that wasn't possible. Not when her parents still panicked every time she coughed, while her siblings still treated her as if she was made of glass, while Dean still treated her as something to protect for ever.

All this she thought in one appalling moment as she stared at Sam and thought, *How did he know?*

She'd come all the way to Queensland because no one here would know. She'd be normal.

Even her car… Her parents had mortgaged everything to cover her medical treatment and she'd ask them for nothing more. Adults bought their own cars, and she was an independent adult. This was her life now, to do with what she wanted.

And she wasn't a renal patient.

'I'm sorry,' Sam said, and she knew he was reading her face. 'Doug and I saw the scar last night, so of course I checked out your arms.'

Of course.

She was so careful. She wore long-sleeved shirts to cover the scars from years of dialysis, and she'd never voluntarily show anyone the unmistakeable renal scar that ran from behind her arm to under her breastbone. But she hadn't been careful when faced with a dying dog. She'd taken off her shirt to treat Bonnie, and she was paying the price now.

'I'm fine now,' she managed, and Sam nodded.

'I can see you are, but is this dumb pride thing about the car a matter of declaring your independence to the world?'

'It might be,' she said grudgingly. 'But if it is, I like it. I bought my car with my own money, and after years of being totally dependent on so many people, you have no idea how good that feels. My car's battered and old but it's *my* battered and old. You haven't sent it to the wrecking yard, have you?'

'I wouldn't do that without your permission.'

'You don't have it. I want my car.'

She met his gaze head on. There was a moment's silence, a sort of unspoken battle, and finally he nodded, even conceding a lopsided smile. 'I understand,' he said at last. 'Sort of.'

'Meaning you still think I'm dumb?'

'Meaning you're looking a gift horse in the mouth.'

'You make a pretty sleek gift horse,' she said before she could stop herself. Not the wisest remark.

'Sleek?' he said, sounding bemused.

'It's an impressive suit.'

'Thank you,' he said faintly.

'You're welcome. How do I go about getting my car back?'

'I'll get it for you. But I *will* clean it.'

'I'll let you do that.'

'That's big of you,' he said, and she smiled.

'Sorry. Thank you. It was an amazing gesture. Really generous.'

'I would like to do something more for you than cleaning your car.'

'You can. Don't tell anyone about the renal transplant.'

'I won't, but tell me…how long ago?'

'Three years.'

'You talk as if it was a long-term problem.'

She sighed. She didn't want to talk about it but she'd already snubbed this man. He was a doctor and he was curious, and he'd promised to keep her secret.

'I had an infection when I was eight, and things pretty much went downhill from there,' she told him. 'I had a transplant at fifteen, but it failed. The second one worked. I had it three years ago and it's been a major, unbelievable success.

'The doctors are telling me to get on with my life, I'm cured, so that's exactly what I'm doing. I have my whole life ahead of me and I'm planning to enjoy every minute of it. If you knew the things I've dreamed, things I can now do…'

But he was into practicalities, not dreams. 'Three years…' He frowned. 'When did you train as a nurse?'

He was still thinking of her as a renal patient, she thought, and winced. She really didn't want to go further with this conversation. She hated talking about it, but he wasn't asking from idle curiosity. It was friendliness and a bit of professional interest thrown in.

He was…nice, she thought. Gorgeous, too. A girl would be dumb to snub him.

'I trained for ever,' she said briefly. 'It took me seven years, in and out of illness, but for the last two years I've been a hundred per cent well and working full time. I'm normal, and I want to be treated as normal.' She gave him a wry smile. 'So that's where I'm coming from. Accepting a car isn't normal.'

His smile faded. 'I'd have given you the car even if you hadn't had a transplant,' he told her, seriously. 'This car is about my need, not yours.' He paused, as if searching for the right words. 'There are things in my background that make me a bit of a loner,' he said at last. 'I hate being indebted and I feel indebted now. Let me off the hook. Okay, not a car,' he conceded. 'Maybe a car's over the top, but I need to do something. You've just arrived at the hospital. There must be something you need. Furniture for your apartment. Shopping vouchers. Something.'

She opened her mouth to say *'Nothing'*—and then she paused.

She looked at him. She really looked at him.

This guy was a surfer and a consultant. Standing here now, in the sunshine, in the car park of one of Australia's top hospitals, in his gorgeous suit, looking lean, fit and gorgeous, he looked like a guy who had the world at his feet.

He wasn't. Callie had told her his fiancée was dead.

He'd just said he was a bit of a loner and she knew it was true.

She'd spent a long time in dialysis wards. She'd

watched tragedies unfold. She'd seen so many of her renal-patient friends struggle with always being the recipient of help, never being able to give back. Bad things happened, she thought as she watched him, and when bad things happened, good people helped. But it was one of the hardest things in the world to keep on taking.

That was part of what this car was about, she thought. This guy would have done his share of taking, and taking sympathy was especially hard. Sam would have had to take again last night when she'd been the only one there to help. The shock must have hauled him straight back to the time his fiancée had died—and she knew suddenly that he needed to give back in order to right his world. Loner or not, he had to do something for her to repay the balance.

She didn't know how she knew it but she did. This man was hurting.

She glanced again at the car he was offering. If she was really generous she'd accept it, she thought ruefully, and in a weird way the thought made sense to her. It'd leave him as a loner. It'd give her a good car.

Only she wasn't generous enough. She wanted her own little car. It meant too much to her.

There must be something you need...

What? She stood in the warm Queensland sun and watched this man with his sun-bleached hair and his crinkled eyes and thought.

'There is something,' she said slowly. 'Something I would really, really appreciate.'

She saw his face clear and she knew she'd been right. He needed to do this.

So say it, she told herself and she did.

'I'd like you to teach me how to surf.'

* * *

Whoa.

Teach her to surf? Was she kidding?

Last night the thought of buying her a car had seemed brilliant. The girl was a needy new arrival to town and she'd saved his dog. He wanted to do something big for her, to show her how much he appreciated her help, and then he wanted to walk away. If she'd taken it, he could have handed her the keys, felt a warm glow every time he saw her car in the car park and think he'd paid for Bonnie's life with a bruised cheek and a small dent in his bank balance.

He wasn't being let off so easily.

He did not want to teach this woman to surf. He didn't want to teach anyone to surf.

Surfing was his personal space. Since Emily had died he'd surfed almost every day. It was a ritual, a space where he could be totally alone, focussed only on the waves. The surf was the place and time where the demons that had haunted him since Emily had died finally let him be.

He didn't know why, but he'd loved surfing before he'd met Emily and he loved it even after her death.

He'd taught Emily to surf.

But Emily's death was nothing to do with this woman, he told himself. That was no reason to knock back her request. Surely he no longer needed to be so isolated, to surf until he was so tired at night that he finally slept, to have time when he could block out the judgement in his head.

She was watching him, waiting for his response. Reading his expression?

'It's okay,' she said quickly, taking a step back. 'It's no big deal. I told you, you don't owe me. Tell Bonnie to visit and give me a big lick when she's better. That's all the thanks I need. Now, where can I find my car?'

'I'll find someone to teach you to surf.'

'Thank you,' she said stiffly.

'I'm not a good teacher.'

'And I'm not a good surfer, but we both know it's not about that,' she said. 'You don't want anyone in your personal space, just like I don't want anyone pushing into my independence.'

'That's not what this is about.'

'I think it is,' she said softly. 'It's okay, Sam. Callie told me about your fiancée. You saw my scars, I guess I'm seeing yours as well. So let's respect them. My dream is to be independent, yours is to crawl into your shell and stay there. So let's just leave it at that. You don't mess with me and I won't mess with you.'

And unbelievably she reached out and touched him lightly on the back of his hand, the faintest of touches, a moment of connection…

'Leave it,' she said softly. 'It was a pleasure to help and that's it.'

And she turned and started walking away.

'Zoe?'

'It's fine.'

'Zoe!' It was practically a yell and she stilled and turned. One eyebrow rose in a faint, quizzical look that was almost a smile. As if she was teasing.

Teasing… It needed only that.

'Yes,' he said.

'Yes?'

'Yes, I'll teach you to surf.'

His words were too loud. They resonated around the car park, and he thought there was no way he could take them back.

He wanted to, but they were out there.

There was a moment's silence while she watched him. The teasing had faded.

'That sounds more like, yes, you'll teach me to walk on nails and you'll be forced to demonstrate first. It sounds like it'll hurt.'

'It won't hurt.'

'It sounds like it'll hurt.'

'It won't hurt,' he exploded, and she took another step back—and suddenly she grinned.

She thought this was funny?

'I'm pushing your buttons,' she told him. 'It's okay, really. I'm not intending to intrude. I've always thought it'd be cool, but I wasn't even able to swim until two years ago. I've been so conscious of infection. But for the last two years I've swum every day, pushing myself. That's part of the reason I moved here, for the sun and the beach. I do want to learn to surf, but you don't have to teach me. As you said, there are other teachers. You can recommend someone or I'll ask around.' She smiled at him then, and it was a kindly smile. 'Let me know when my car's ready. See you later, Sam, and thank you.'

And she turned again and walked away, definitely, surely, putting distance between them with every step.

He stood and watched her. She was a nurse in a nurse's uniform. From the back she looked like any other nurse.

Just a woman. Nothing special.

But she was special. That's what scared him.

He was being selfish and dumb and emotional and there was no need to be. He could teach this woman to surf. He could give her a few impersonal lessons on the beach, get her to the stage where she could surf in the safe, rookie areas, and then leave her to it. What was the big deal?

She'd almost reached the hospital entrance. She was nothing but a nurse, moving away.

She'd saved his dog. That was all. This was a debt he needed to repay, and he would, whether she wanted it or not.

'Yes,' he called out, and she paused but didn't turn.

'Nails,' she called back, and started walking again.

'It's not nails. It could even be fun.'

She turned again then and looked at him. She was a hundred yards from him. Distant. Impersonal. A medical colleague.

From here he couldn't see the twinkle in those gorgeous, violet-blue eyes. From here he couldn't see if she was still laughing at him.

He suspected she was.

'Fun?' she called.

This was dumb, having a conversation so far apart. People were streaming in and out of the entrance. A couple of colleagues looked at Sam and looked at Zoe and then looked at Sam again, and he could see the questions growing.

Get this over with and get out of here.

'Bonnie will be at the vet's all weekend,' he called. 'First lesson Sunday. Meet me at two o'clock, here.'

'Really?'

'Yes,' he called, goaded. 'And your car will be ready by then, too.'

'Wow!'

Even a hundred yards apart he could see her face split into a grin so wide it was like the sun had come out. A brilliant sun. Cade Coleman, the hospital's new neonatal specialist, a guy Sam was only just getting to know but who had already created sizzle among the hospital's female staff, had just emerged from the entrance. Cade paused and smiled at Zoe's gorgeous grin—well, who wouldn't?—and Sam had an almost irresistible urge to stride forward and claim the grin as his own.

To claim the woman as his own?

How dumb was that? Somehow he forced his feet not to move. He needed to climb into his own car and go find the dealer he'd left Zoe's car with. He also had a long ward round to do before he could spend some time with Bonnie.

'Two o'clock, then,' he forced himself to call to Zoe, and she waved and grinned some more.

'I'll bring snacks,' she called. 'I'm feeling homesick and when I'm homesick I cook. I'll make lamingtons.'

'You can make lamingtons?' Cade demanded, and Sam watched his colleague move in, smoothly smiling, laughing with Zoe. They turned and walked back into the hospital and Sam stood in the car park and thought…he'd just lost something.

That was an even dumber thought. He had nothing to lose.

Except a dog, he reminded himself. He needed to go and see how she was. He needed to haul himself together and remember priorities and put the thought of one beaming smile behind him.

He needed to pay his debt and get the connection with Zoe behind him.

'Sam Webster bought you a car?'

Zoe had walked out of the lift, turned the first bend in the corridor—and run straight into Callie Richards.

She stopped dead when she saw Zoe, and Zoe had no choice but to stop, too. Who else knew about the car?

'Yes.'

'And you knocked him back and now he's teaching you to surf?'

'Okay, I give up,' Zoe said, exasperated. 'Do you guys have the parking lot bugged for sound?'

Callie chuckled. 'No need. Don't tell me Adelaide South is any different. Hospital staff have their own specialist spy network, which beams gossip around the hospital before it even happens.'

'I guess.' Zoe gave a rueful grin. 'Adelaide South was small, though. I hoped Gold Coast City might be more impersonal.'

'Fat hope,' Callie said. 'How are you feeling?'

'I'm fine.'

'Be careful of Cade Coleman.'

She frowned. 'What?'

'He's new, from the States, but he comes with a health warning. Breaker of hearts.'

'I talked to him for two minutes,' Zoe said, astounded. 'I'd have thought you might have warned me about Sam.'

'I don't need to warn you about Sam. There's no way anyone's going to break through that impervious barrier.'

There was a moment's loaded silence. Then...

'Is there anyone else I need to watch out for?' Zoe demanded. She'd tried—and failed—not to sound snappy but she couldn't help herself. This woman was a senior physician. Warning nurses about consultants wouldn't be in her job description. On top of that, Callie normally seemed reserved. Zoe was starting to suspect what was going on, and she didn't like it.

'I'm sorry. I know it's none of my business,' Callie said. 'It's just…'

'Just that you've read my personnel records?' Zoe ventured, and Callie looked a bit nonplussed. Then she shrugged.

'You've come to work on my ward, Zoe. I check my staff from the ground up.'

'So you've read about my renal transplant—and you think I need looking out for?'

'Okay, backing off now,' Callie said, and held up her hands in mock surrender. 'Yes, I read your records. I was on the selection committee and it's my job. I knew a transplant wouldn't impede your work and I put it to one side. But of course I didn't forget. Then when you came in last night covered in blood, my mother-hen instincts took over.' Her smile was beguiling, appealing for forgiveness. 'I don't normally do the mother-hen thing,' she confessed. 'It was a momentary weakness and I apologise. If you fancy Cade Coleman—or indeed Sam Webster—then you go, girl.'

It was impossible to be angry in the face of that smile—and the in the face of an apology for what, after all, was only care. 'It's okay,' Zoe said, her anger fading. 'As long as the whole world doesn't know about the transplant. Now Sam knows…'

'Sam knows?'

'He saw my scars yesterday, but he's promised to keep it to himself. If it's possible in this hospital.'

'It's possible. Only the head of each unit has access to records. It won't go past me. Or Sam.'

'Thank you.'

'So are you interested?' Callie said, relaxing a bit.

'In who?'

'Either of 'em.'

'No!' Zoe said. She hesitated but this woman had been good to her. Why not say it like it was? 'I went out with the same boy for more than ten years. He wrapped me up in cotton wool so tight I couldn't breathe. Now I'm breathing just as hard as I can, and I don't want a relationship.'

'Good for you,' Callie said. 'Men!'

And Zoe thought of Callie's comment about working in the women's refuge.

'They're useful, though,' Callie conceded. 'Love 'em and leave 'em. There's a good rule in life. Enjoy your surfing with Sam, and anything else that comes along.'

'Thank you,' Zoe said, and watched Callie head round the bend to the lift.

She thought, Yes, I will.

She shouldn't have said anything.

The last thing Callie Richards thought of herself as was a mother hen. She had a reputation for staying aloof, and normally she did.

It was just that something last night had touched her. One bloodied, bedraggled girl whose medical history said she'd been to death's door and back.

That, and knowing Cade Coleman was on her patch.

She hadn't even met the guy but his reputation had preceded him. His stepbrother, Alex, had rung her and asked if there was a vacancy.

'He's a fine neonatal physician, Callie. The best. He's looking for a complete break, so he wants to move from the States. Queensland would be prefect. If you have room on your team...'

She had. And Cade's qualifications were impressive, to say the least.

There'd been one caveat. Women.

The man was running, Alex had told her. Personal stuff. Problems. Callie hadn't pushed and Alex hadn't offered more, except to say they were 'worse than mine'. For Alex, that was really saying something. The time between Alex and her…

Yeah, well, block that out. She put it aside deliberately now, and thought of the good stuff. Cade's qualifications outweighed any potential womanising.

But he'd arrived yesterday and already there was a ripple doing the rounds about how good-looking he was.

Forget it, she told herself harshly. On Monday she'd meet him and see just how good a doctor he was. Meanwhile…

Yeah, warning Zoe had seemed over the top, but Ros had seen Cade talking to her and had reported it with excitement.

'Our new nurse has just found our new physician. Ooh, I do love a good bit of intrigue. Bring it on.'

So she'd overreacted. Cade was probably harmless, she conceded, and as for warning Zoe over one chance meeting…

Ridiculous.

She took a deep breath, turned toward the lift—and Cade Coleman was right in front of her.

He was standing by the lifts, his hand on the buttons as if he'd pushed more than once and was getting irritated. As well he might, Callie conceded. The lifts in this building were notoriously slow.

How long had he been standing there?

'Hi,' she managed, and put out a hand in welcome. 'I'm Callie Richards.'

'Yeah, the woman who hired me.' He was tall, over

six feet or so, tanned, lean and ripped. He'd just flown halfway round the world but if he was suffering from jet lag he certainly didn't show it.

What he was suffering from, though, was anger. She could feel it coming from him in waves.

'I didn't hire you,' she managed evenly. 'I just recommended you to the powers that be.'

'Because Alex recommended me to you.'

'I know Alex,' she said evenly. 'We've worked together. His word—that you're the best—was good enough for me.'

'So good that you need to put out a warning to the nursing staff?'

He had heard.

'I'm so sorry.' There was no getting out of this one. She felt like turning and running but his anger kept her locked in. 'I thought…shift change is over. There's never anyone around.'

'We all have apartments on this floor, it seems,' he said, icy cold. 'I came up in the lift with Zoe—all the way, without seducing her once. The key Admin gave me for my apartment worked when I first arrived but it doesn't work now. Neither does this elevator.'

As if on cue, the lift arrived. The doors slid open.

Callie wanted to get in, but Cade was blocking her way.

'So why am I so dangerous?' he demanded, tossing his useless key in the air and catching it again. He seemed dangerous, Callie thought. Lean, mean and dangerous to know.

'You're not. It's just…Zoe's been unwell.'

'A renal transplant. I heard. And she doesn't want it known but your carrying voice took it all the way to here.'

'You shouldn't have been listening.'

'You want me to block my ears in my own apartment building?'

'I'm sorry,' she said again.

'Not good enough. Tell me why the warning.' It was almost a growl.

She took a deep breath. Wow, Alex had really landed her in it with this one. She'd greeted his call querying work for his brother with pleasure and she hadn't expected to land in it up to her neck.

This was Alex's call, she decided. Not hers.

'Alex told me you were the best neonatal physician he knew,' she said. 'I respect that. He also said you'd had trouble with women.'

'Did he just?' He practically snarled. 'Generous of him. Well, you needn't worry. Your sick little nurse is safe from me.'

'Zoe's not sick—and I've said I'm sorry. If you have any argument, take it up with your brother, not me. Now, if you don't mind, I need to get back to the wards. Only I'm taking the stairs.'

And she turned on her heel and stalked to the fire exit, thinking four floors of stairs was a small price to pay.

Sam had two patients to see and then he was free for the day. Or almost. He emerged from his consulting rooms to find Cade Coleman waiting for him. Looking furious.

For a moment Sam thought about his ridiculous reaction as he'd seen Cole in the entrance with Zoe. His response had been almost primeval—wanting to go and claim this woman as his. It had been dumb and irrelevant, and nothing to do with his new colleague. But why was Cole looking at him so angrily?

'Not guilty?' he tried. This guy had only been here since yesterday. The hospital bigwigs had been delighted to hire him, and for good reason. Sam had been the one elected to meet him at the airport and he'd spoken to him a couple of times since. Already they were planning research projects. This guy was seriously smart.

This guy looked like he was about to punch a hole in the wall and then get on a plane back to the States.

'Dr Richards,' he said through gritted teeth.

'Callie?' Sam tried for a smile. 'What's she done to upset you? The lady's one classy doctor.'

'Who's warning the female staff that I eat them for breakfast.'

'What's she doing that for?'

'She saw me talking to your nurse.'

'My nurse?' God, this hospital grapevine. 'You mean Zoe?'

'Apparently it's a wonder I didn't grope her in the elevator.'

'What the hell has got into Callie?'

'She might,' Cade admitted, 'have been warned by my brother.'

'Right,' Sam said, steering for safe ground but not quite knowing in what direction it was. 'So your brother warned Callie that you grope nurses in lifts?'

He met Cade's angry gaze head on, his own expression noncommittal, doctor calmly asking colleague whether he ate nurses for breakfast. Cade's glare faded in the face of calm enquiry, and he shrugged, and in the end even managed a rueful smile.

'I guess you never know with Americans,' he said.

'There was a phrase the Aussie guys used for the Yanks when you lot were out here during the war,' Sam said mildly. 'Overpaid, oversexed and over here. Maybe Callie has a residual phobia.' He sighed. 'Look, Zoe's new here—'

'And I know about the renal transplant.'

'How the hell did that get around the hospital?'

'Your Dr Richards,' Cade said, his anger surfacing again. Then, as he saw Sam's face and maybe saw the anger beginning to surface there as well, he shook his head. 'It's okay. I know your lady wants to keep it private. You'll note I made sure there's no one in earshot now.'

'She's not my lady.'

'She's not mine either,' Cade said. 'I didn't touch her and I don't intend to touch her, so if you could tell Dr Richards to keep out of my face...'

'I'll talk to her.' This conversation was weird. What was going on with Callie?

'Excellent,' Cade said, calming down. 'See to it. I'm here to do a job. I don't care what bee Dr Richards has in her bonnet, but I'm not a woman-eater. Nurse Zoe is all yours.'

And he turned and stalked away, leaving Sam staring after him.

Nurse Zoe is all yours...

Not in a million years, he thought.

Except he had to teach her to surf.

Why was it worrying him so much? Why did he feel this was a huge mistake?

It was the way she made him feel, he thought, and he had to do something about that. Once upon a time he'd been engaged to be married and if that was where his judgement took him…never again.

Teach the lady to surf and move on.

CHAPTER FOUR

SAM WORKED MOST of Saturday. It was supposed to be his time off, but medical imperatives didn't necessarily fit around weekends. When a baby was admitted with a major heart abnormality early on Saturday morning there was no choice but to abandon his plan to spend the day with Bonnie, and instead concentrate on saving Joshua Bennet's life.

Operating on a baby as frail as Joshua was fraught, the odds seemed stacked against them, but Sam's team was seriously good. Luck played out on their side and by the time he walked out of Theatre at six o'clock he felt like Joshua had every chance of making it to a ripe old age.

He also felt seriously wiped.

Callie found him at the sinks. She was a mate, a real friend, and she walked straight up and gave him a hug.

He wouldn't accept a hug from anyone else, but Callie Richards wasn't one to hold back. She'd known him since training. She'd been there when Emily had died and the armour he'd put up around himself didn't stop her pushing the boundaries.

'That was magnificent, Sam,' she told him. 'I've just seen Josh's mum. She can't stop crying, and for good reason. She knew the odds.'

'This is a great team,' he said gruffly, extricating himself, fighting back emotion and finding a safe retreat. 'Um…Callie, what's the deal with the new guy? Cade?'

'Yeah, I may have stuffed that up,' Callie said. 'A bit of overreaction. I went into protection mode with your Zoe.'

There it was again. Your Zoe.

'She's not,' he said pleasantly, but with a hint of steel behind the words, 'my Zoe.'

'Of course not,' Callie said, and had the temerity to chuckle. 'But you have to admit she's cute. And you gave her a car and now you're giving her surfing lessons. For lone wolf Sam to get that involved…'

'It's just a thank-you gesture,' he said stiffly. 'A couple of hours' surfing every Sunday and nothing more.'

'Yeah, well, good luck with that. I've known her for all of a week and already I'm seeing she's special. She's brilliant on the wards—skilled but also incredibly empathetic with the kids and their parents. She seems to make people relax, taking the fear out of this place. And if she can make sick kids relax…beware, Sam.'

'Callie…'

'Yeah, it's not my business,' she said, and grinned and backed off. 'Just saying. Two hours' surfing every Sunday? Hmm. This hospital's a fish bowl, Sam Webster. You spend two hours with her and then try and avoid her for the rest of the time…well, there's not far you can go, working here. You'll hit the walls and bounce right back. Zoe's a solid part of our paediatric team. She's already proved she's your friend and from where I'm standing I'd like her to have a chance of being even more than that to one of my favourite colleagues.'

* * *

This hospital!

It drove him nuts, Sam thought as he headed for the vet's to see Bonnie. Gossip, matchmaking, innuendo…

He'd moved here from Perth after Emily had died, wanting a clean break, wanting to work in an environment where no one knew his story and he could retire into his seclusion of work and surfing. But, of course, Australia may be geographically big but in terms of population it was a small country, and the medical community was even smaller. He'd walked into the wards on the first day and met Callie, a doctor he'd trained with. The chief theatre nurse had spent time in Perth and knew Emily and her story. The janitor, a kite-surfing nut, had been a volunteer lifeguard on the Perth beach the day Emily had died.

So much for anonymity. But until now he'd kept his distance. Callie had fretted at the edges but he didn't want her concern. He didn't want anyone's concern. He just wanted to get on with life on his terms. Medicine, surfing—and Bonnie.

He felt his pulse rate rise a bit as he pulled into the vet's parking lot. He'd been in touch all day but still it'd be good to see his dog for himself.

She was twelve years old. He had to lose her one day, but not yet. Please, not yet. He should have been here sooner, he told himself harshly, but there'd been no time. He'd organised Zoe's car in brief intervals between work commitments, but his tiny patient Joshua couldn't have been set aside so he could be with his dog.

Still, the thought that she was here, in the recovery room at the vet's, probably alone, had eaten at him, and his stride became a run as he headed up the steps to the entrance. The receptionist smiled at him and motioned him to go through into the recovery area.

He swung through the door. 'Bonnie's in the end cage,' the receptionist had said, and his eyes went straight to the end of the room—and saw Zoe Payne crouched in front of the floor-level cage. The cage door was open and Bonnie was half in, half out of the cage.

Her great soft head was lying on Zoe's lap.

Girl and dog.

Neither girl nor dog had heard the doors swing open. Bonnie seemed asleep. Zoe was turned away from him. She was simply dressed in jeans and soft cotton shirt, with her hair loosely caught back in a bouncy ponytail. He could just see the profile of her face.

She was talking to Bonnie.

'He's agreed to teach me to surf, and I need you to help. I'm a bit scared of the big boards. It's always seemed magic—you must love it too, watching it night after night. But do you know what I've done? I found a discount store today and they sell all sorts of flags. They're actually Tibetan prayer flags, so I'm thinking they'll give you even more safety—almost a blessing as you watch us surf. They're attached to long poles and I'm going to stick them in the sand right where you lie so people can see for miles that someone very special is snoozing in the sand. That would be you. You get that leg better and we'll make the beach safe so you can live happily ever after.'

What was it with this girl? Sam thought numbly. What was it that made his heart clench?

He didn't want this feeling. He didn't want to feel like he wanted to walk forward, crouch down and hug the pair of them.

How could he stop wanting?

'How long does it take to learn to surf?' Zoe was asking Bonnie now. 'How long does it take before I'll be brave enough to catch one of those gorgeous, curling waves that loop right over? I want that so much.'

She wanted the big waves—and that was enough to make things right themselves. Any thought of hugging went right out the window. This woman wanted what had killed Emily.

He knew it wasn't the same, yet it was enough for him to haul himself together, remind himself that this was a professional colleague and their only personal connection would be a two-hour surfing lesson each Sunday. He pinned a smile on his face and walked forward, allowing his feet to make a sound on the tiled floor so she heard him and looked up.

She smiled a greeting and that was enough to set him back again.

Professional. Colleagues.

She had his dog's head on her knee.

'Hey,' she said softly. 'I hope you don't mind. I just popped in to check, and Doug said it'd be okay.'

'I don't mind at all,' he said, crouching beside her, and there was another jolt. What was it with this woman—the way she made him feel? He did not want this. 'Thank you for caring.'

'I love dogs,' she said. 'I've always wanted one. My parents said they had germs.'

'Maybe I can buy you a puppy instead of a car.'

'No way,' she said, fondling the sleeping Bonnie's ears in a way that made him feel…odd. Needful? Weird. 'The deal is surfing lessons. I'm living in a hospital apartment, working long shifts. That's no life for a puppy—even if I did get permission to keep a dog. I don't know how you managed it.'

'Deal breaker,' he said. 'Gold Coast offered me a job. I said it's me and Bonnie or neither of us. We come as a package deal and they accepted.'

'I would have thought a little house with a back yard might be better for her.'

'Believe it or not, the apartment's better. I couldn't get a house within five minutes' drive of the hospital so Bonnie would be left alone all day. As it is, I can take her out to the foreshore three or four times a day instead of taking coffee breaks, and she's even found herself a job in the wards.'

'As a companion dog,' Zoe said, her hands still doing that gentle stroking. 'Callie says she's great.'

Bonnie hadn't moved. The painkillers would still have her heavily sedated, but even so…why would she move when she was lying on Zoe's knee? Why would anyone move?

It was strange, sitting on the floor of the vet's recovery room, with this woman and his dog. A cat was snoozing down the far end of the room, and above them a fat snake was lazing in a heated tank. The snake had some type of dressing round its rear end. Weird, Sam thought, and wondered idly how a vet would treat the heart of a snake.

'How would you go about putting an aortic stent into that?' Zoe asked, following his gaze.

How did she do that? It was like she could read his thoughts.

Nonsense—it was coincidence and nothing else.

'I reckon if I had a snake with heart disease I might buy another snake,' he told her.

'Like you'd buy another Labrador?'

'Different thing.'

'Not to the owner of the snake,' she said. 'Love's where you find it.'

'That sounds like something my grandma might say.'

'Does your grandma like snakes?'

'Excluding snakes,' he said, and grinned. 'You can't cuddle a snake.'

'Yeah, love needs cuddles,' she said, and bent and cuddled Bonnie some more, and there was all sorts of stuff happening in his chest and he didn't want any of it. 'Sam…'

'Mmm?' He'd like to back out of here, he thought. He needed to leave and come back when this woman wasn't here. It was bad enough that he'd nearly lost his dog, but the way Bonnie was lying there, it was like…he was losing her a little anyway. Giving part of her to Zoe.

Jealous?

No. It wasn't jealousy, he thought. It was sharing, and he didn't do sharing. Sharing meant…sharing. Since Emily's death he carefully hadn't shared anything at all.

'Doug said she'll need to stay off her leg for weeks,' she said. 'Even though it's plated, he wants the bone fragments to have every chance they can get to fuse. I was thinking…if you wanted to share care, I go onto night duty on Monday. Bonnie could stay with you during the night, but you could pop her into my apartment during the day. You need to sleep at night. I need to sleep during the day. Bonnie needs to sleep all the time but you can't tell me she won't sleep better in a basket right next to a human. I know you're best but for the next few days, would you like me to be second best?'

Whoa.

Say no, he told himself fiercely. He did not want to be further indebted.

The trouble was, she was right. Bonnie wasn't just suffering from a broken leg. The lacerations were deep and nasty, she had fractured ribs and she had massive bruising. Even though the plate would allow her to weight-bear almost immediately, she'd still need to be kept quiet.

For her to sleep by Zoe during the day…

'Just add another surfing lesson to the end of my course,' Zoe said, smiling at him. 'But, honestly, it'll be as much for me as it is for Bonnie. I've never lived away from home before. I wanted to come here, but I am lonely.'

Help.

He wasn't used to this. Emily would never have looked at him frankly and admitted loneliness. Admitting weakness was…weak.

Maybe it wasn't. There wasn't much about Zoe that spelled weakness, he thought. She was direct and honest, and she was waiting for an answer to an offer that made sense.

'Thank you,' he said, because he had no choice, and she gave a businesslike nod that said her offer had no emotional overtones at all, that it was all about sense.

'Excellent. Would you like to slide in here under Bonnie?'

As if on cue, his dog opened her eyes and looked at him. He'd been expecting her to look like she was in pain, shocked, confused. Instead…she almost looked smug, as though to say, 'I have the two of you at my disposal. You want to get this shift change over fast so I can go back to my comfortable snooze?'

He sat beside Zoe, she eased back and handed over her position, but as she did, his body brushed hers, his hands touched hers, and she was so close…

And then she moved away.

'Bye, Bonnie,' Zoe whispered. 'You keep on getting better. Bye, Sam. See you tomorrow.'

And she was gone.

She wasn't imposing, he thought. She'd come to see Bonnie but she had no intention of interfering with his time with her.

It'd be okay. He could share Bonnie's care with her for the next few weeks, and he could teach her to surf, because she'd respect his boundaries. He could tell that about her already.

The problem was…

'The problem is that I don't know where those boundaries are any more,' he told Bonnie, but Bonnie was already asleep again.

Bonnie was happy. Bonnie was safe and settled, and he should feel good.

He did feel good. He just didn't feel…settled.

He approached Sunday with a certain amount of trepidation, but it wasn't justified.

What had he expected? Some needy kid, giggling, treating it as a joke? Or—and subconsciously maybe this was what he'd most feared—a woman treating it as a first date? An excuse to get close, as so many woman had tried to since Emily's death.

He knew he had been seen as fair game by the single female staff since Emily had died, and maybe he'd been expecting the same from Zoe.

But she wasn't the least bit interested. She made that clear from the outset when she ran out to the parking lot to meet him, carting an armload of wetsuit and a box full of lamingtons. She was wearing faded shorts and a rash vest, she'd hauled her hair back into a loose knot to get it out of the way and her face was coated in thick, white zinc.

No woman he knew wore the practical, sensible but thick and obvious white zinc sunscreen. Better a bit of sunburn than sporting a pure white nose, but Zoe appeared oblivious.

'Callie lent me her wetsuit,' she told him. 'I'll buy my own as soon as I'm assured this sport's not going to humiliate me.'

She had no time for niceties, for social chitchat. He'd promised her two hours and she was intent on taking every single moment of those two hours and using them to full effect. They spent the first hour on the beach, practising lying full length on the board then doing the seemingly simple yet vital sweep to standing. He told her what to do, he helped her, he corrected her, he held her while she balanced, and there was no hint she even saw him as a person.

He was the conduit to her surfing, and she ached to surf.

When he finally told her she'd graduated to the shallows her beam was almost house-wide, but it wasn't for him. She was totally inward-focussed, and by the time the two hours were up he knew that she was fulfilling a dream she'd had for years. It was as though she was watching a rainbow and having someone steer the boat while she headed for it. All eyes were on the rainbow.

So there, he told himself ruefully as they hauled the

surfboards up the beach at the end of the two hours and hit the box of lamingtons with relish. Zoe had managed to do a wobbly stand in six inches of water, but by her beaming grin you'd have thought she'd conquered twenty-foot boomers.

'It was awesome,' she said, smiling and smiling.

'So are these lamingtons.'

'Thank you.'

'I'll be down on the beach tomorrow night if you want to come,' he heard himself say—and then did a double-take inside. Had he really said that?

But she was shaking her head.

'Night duty tomorrow,' she said. 'I don't want to start tired. Plus I need to decorate my room. I have so many plans, you can't imagine. Besides, this is your time, your surfing. I don't want to interfere with your private space. Two hours on Sunday is all I ask, and it's all I'll take. Thank you, Sam, for a magic two hours.'

And she heaved her surfboard—one she'd hired at his suggestion until they could figure what would suit her—on top of her battered little car before he could help her, tied it down with clinical efficiency, gave him a wave and another of her bright smiles, and left him.

She'd gone, and the beach was emptier for her going.

Well, of course it was, he told himself savagely. What was he, an idiot? Why was he standing looking after her like a teenage kid with a crush?

He had another couple of hours before he needed to get back to the real world. Bonnie would be discharged from the vet's tomorrow. This might be the last chance for weeks to have a really solid surf.

He hauled himself together and headed back to the waves, but the thought of Zoe stayed with him.

He didn't need to worry about boundaries, he thought. *I have so many plans, you can't imagine...* Surfing was simply one of them and any thought that she'd see him as part of those plans was pure ego.

Or pure desire?

There was definitely desire. Sense or not, she'd left him with half a box of lamingtons—and he wanted more.

He didn't see her all Monday. Even if he'd wanted, he had no time to see her. He, Cade and Callie treated Molly Carthardy, aged four, who presented with shortness of breath at kindergarten. The kindergarten teacher had queried asthma but Molly had ended up on the operating table getting a full graft to replace a faulty artery. She'd make it, which made Sam smile, and he was left seriously impressed with Cade's skills. Great colleagues or not, though, he left work exhausted. Then he collected Bonnie and brought her home.

She was sore and sorry for herself but she could walk with a heavy limp, and she was overjoyed to be back with him, back in her own basket.

He spent the night with her, carrying her outside twice so she could sniff the grass in the small entrance garden. At seven in the morning he needed to be back in the wards, and Bonnie whined as he dressed—she knew what his suit and tie meant. Zoe's offer was there. It was sensible and Bonnie came before pride. 'It's only a couple more surfing lessons and you're worth it,' he told her, and he picked up the gear she'd need for the day and went and knocked on Zoe's apartment door.

Zoe answered with the smile that did his head in.

It was the beam he was starting to know—and love? It was like the sun had come out, radiating straight from that smile.

'Hey, I hoped you'd take me up on my offer.' But she wasn't beaming at him. She was hugging Bonnie, who gave a little snort of pleasure and shoved her nose into Zoe's armpit.

Zoe had obviously just come off night shift, showered and changed into sleeping gear. Her gorgeous curls were spiralling, damp and wild, down her back. She was wearing a vast, soft, powder-blue dressing gown, which looked like it'd fit two of her in it, and he had an almost irresistible desire to see if two would fit.

Dog-girl greeting over, Zoe looked up at him and he almost had his face under control by the time she did.

'If you meant your offer…'

'Of course I meant my offer. You've brought her stuff—great.'

'I've just taken her outside. She should be right to sleep for hours.'

'I never sleep well anyway,' she confessed. 'I get up and snack, so if I need to get up and take Bonnie outside it won't affect me at all. Do you have a number I can reach you on if I need you?'

'I… Sure.' He waited while she grabbed a pen and then watched in astonishment as she scrawled it on her hand.

'There,' she said. 'May I never need to wash again.' Then she chuckled. 'Okay, I'm a nurse, I need to wash, but one of the hospital techies is fixing my phone. I'll get it back tonight and then you can have your own permanent place in my friends' list.'

And what was there in that statement to make him feel uncomfortable? To feel like he was stepping over boundaries? A colleague, putting his cellphone number in her list of contacts? What was weird about that?

'Hey, don't look like that,' she told him, and this time, thankfully, she hadn't read his thoughts, or if she'd tried, she'd got it wrong. 'I know it must be awful leaving Bonnie but she's in safe hands. I won't let her on my bed—I won't let her risk her leg by jumping. If she gets distressed I might even drag my mattress onto the floor. Bonnie and I intend to have a lovely, cosy time, don't we, Bon? She'll be safe, Sam. I will look after her and I don't take risks.'

And there it was.

I don't take risks.

What was it in that statement that made his world change?

She was a gorgeous, warm, vibrant, clever, kind, resourceful woman, and she was standing in front of him, declaring that she didn't take risks.

A knot inside him seemed to be unravelling.

Something inside him was saying that maybe he could just…take a risk himself?

'Go,' she said, and suddenly, before he knew what she intended, she straightened, stood on tiptoe and kissed him, lightly, on the cheek. 'Off you go to save the world while woman and dog keep the home fires burning. Work well while we sleep well.'

And then she ushered Bonnie into her apartment, she gathered Bonnie's bedding from his seemingly limp arms, she gave him another of her gorgeous smiles—and she backed inside and closed the door behind her.

Zoe closed the door, stooped to comfort a worried Bonnie, and then found herself leaning against the

door as if the weight of her body could stop it opening again. As if she should lean against it and keep Dr
Sam Webster on the other side.

There were two Sam Websters, she thought, trying
to catch her breath. One was the guy who surfed. He
was lean, bronzed and ripped, with sun-bleached hair
and eyes the colour of the sea. The other was the chief
paediatric cardiologist of Gold Coast City Hospital,
a skilled, empathetic surgeon at the top of his game.
She'd been here long enough to learn Sam's reputation
was second to none. The package of Cardiologist Sam
included sleek Italian suits, the faint scent of mascu-
line aftershave and gorgeous silk ties. His tie was dot-
ted with embroidered teddy bears this morning, and
had seemed enough to make her go weak at the knees.

'It's not fair,' she told Bonnie, letting go of the emotions she'd been fiercely repressing from the time she'd
heard the doorbell. She felt herself blush from the toes
up. 'Whoa, this is my teenage years catching up with
me. All those times while my sisters had adolescent
fancies and I was too sick to join in. I guess I had to
have 'em some time. Here we go. Let's get it all out in
one fell swoop with Dr Sam.'

Three deep breaths. Okay, she was over it, she told
herself as she went back to reassuring Bonnie. Or…
she was sort of over it?

'I shouldn't have kissed him,' she told Bonnie, but
then she thought, no, the kiss was okay. It was the sort
of kiss a woman who wasn't being hormonal would
give; a kiss of friendship and reassurance that she'd
take care of his beloved dog.

She took Bonnie into her bedroom, settled her in
her basket beside the bed and slipped between the
covers. Getting to sleep after night duty, at a time

when the rest of the world was heading to work, was always hard. She'd learned relaxation techniques. She explained them to Bonnie.

'I know you're anxious about being with me and not with Sam, and I know you're sore, but sleep's good. First of all you stretch your toes—or pads. Flex every muscle—only don't flex so far it hurts. Then, tell yourself every single muscle is going to sleep. Focus only on your toes, one after the other. Think of nothing else. Nothing else.'

Silk ties with teddy bears. Aftershave. Sun-creased eyes and a smile to die for.

'See, that's the way to stay awake,' she said crossly to Bonnie, who was showing every sign that the relaxation lecture was working. 'Thinking of Sam. I can think of him and still relax, though. It's sort of like winning Tatts,' she told herself, not very convincingly. 'A girl can dream. As long as you keep those dreams where they belong. Right here on this pillow.'

Bonnie wuffled and stirred and she put her hand down and soothed the soft brown head.

'I know,' she said. 'I'm keeping you awake. I'm stopping now. I can be very sensible when I try.'

She closed her eyes and concentrated on her toes.

Silk ties with teddy bears...

She was going to have to try very hard, she thought. She finally did drift off to sleep but silk ties with teddy bears—and one sexy smile—were right there with her in her dreams.

CHAPTER FIVE

To say Gold Coast City ran on gossip was an understatement. Staff worked long hours under stressful circumstances. The hospital apartments were right next to the hospital, so medics saw each other off duty as well as on. The huge emergency department meant medics and paramedics saw first hand every day how fragile life was. Staff could crack under the pressure, or they could let off steam in other ways, and one of those ways was gossip. Hot affairs were common, but not as common as rumour had it, so Sam shouldn't have been surprised that within two weeks the grapevine had Zoe and him bedded and almost wedded.

The grapevine had played with him before—at one stage he and Callie had been whispered to be a hot item. It hadn't bothered him then that long-term friendship was construed as something else. Callie had almost seemed to enjoy it— 'I'm rumoured to be a bad girl, Sam, so what's a bit more wickedness on the side?' They'd let it run its course and it had done no harm.

So why was the grapevine disturbing him now?

It was because he couldn't step away from her.

Though actually he could. Zoe was on night duty so their paths rarely crossed on the wards. He met her twice a day when he dropped Bonnie off and picked her up. Handover was brief. Zoe always seemed pleased to see him, but maybe she sensed his need to be impersonal. They exchanged a few brief words, an update on how the rapidly recovering Bonnie was faring, and he left as soon as possible.

They had their surfing lessons each Sunday but even then Zoe was so focussed on learning to surf it was as if she hardly noticed him. He'd never seen someone so intent, so determined, and so joyous at each tiny step along the way.

The first time she managed to wobble to her feet and stay upright for a whole ten seconds, a casual observer would have assumed she'd just won Olympic gold for her country. She whooped and whooped, and he had an almost insatiable desire to take her in his arms and lift her and swing her in triumph—and then crush her to him so her triumph was his.

He didn't. He managed to stay back and watch, smiling a little, instructor pleased with student. She looked at him and laughed out loud and kicked and sent a vast spray of water out over him.

'Look at you. You look like I'm pretending to be Einstein because I've just switched on an electric light. I know I have a million miles to go but I've just taken the first step.'

'More than the first step,' he conceded. 'Balancing's hard.'

'It is, isn't it?' she said, and gave a huge, happy sigh and dragged her board back out a little so she could try again. 'Was I standing too far forward? If I go a bit back will I be more stable?'

There it was—the personal moment was over, and they were back to student-teacher.

Impersonal?

He thought of those mornings when he handed Bonnie over, of this girl snuggled in her bathrobe, about to go to bed, and he thought…he thought…

He thought it was just as well she was treating him as a teacher and Bonnie's master and nothing else, because if she made one tentative suggestion that it could be anything more…

Then he'd stand firm, he told himself. He had no choice. He'd been thrown into the chaos of caring once in his life and he had no intention of going there again.

They were colleagues, he thought, with the added dimension that she'd saved his dog and he was teaching her to surf. There was nothing more to it.

Excellent.

But then, two days later, he met her on the wards and things got a bit more complicated.

Ryan Tobin was ten years old and Sam had been worried about him for months now.

He'd first presented with a worsening of what had, until then, seemed mild asthma. Callie had started him on methylprednisone and albuterol but four days later he was back in Emergency, struggling to breathe.

At that stage Callie had called in Sam. A chest radiograph showed an enlarged heart and pulmonary oedema, and from there things had gone from bad to worse.

The diagnosis was dilated cardiomyopathy with non-specific inflammation.

Ryan had spent weeks in and out of hospital, needing oxygen, needing diuretic therapy to ease the oedema. Sam had done everything he could to improve cardiac function, but now…

Sam worked with him for most of the afternoon and into the night, as he finally conceded what he'd worked for months to avoid. The only way for Ryan to live was if he had a transplant.

He'd need to be moved to a hospital where such transplants were performed. They had time; they could get Ryan stable, but Sam couldn't sugar-coat it for his desperate parents. The next few weeks would be touch and go.

At midnight he finally left Ryan's bedside. His parents weren't moving. Ryan's mother was asleep with her head resting on her son's bed, and his father was staring rigidly at the ceiling while he lay on the stretcher bed provided. The hospital encouraged one parent to stay, and while there was no room for two, neither parent intended to leave.

'Tell Mum what's happening. Tell her to take Luke home,' Ryan's father said, and Sam thought of the elderly woman he'd seen day after day in the waiting room, keeping Ryan's eight-year-old brother company.

They'd both seemed stoic. The old lady must be exhausted, Sam thought. If he'd known she was still out there he'd have asked a nurse to see to her hours ago.

But someone was already caring. He walked out of the cardiac care ward, and Ryan's grandma was fast asleep in the waiting room. Someone had hauled out a care chair for her—usually used for patients in terminal care, it was a chair that became a bed and encased its user in a cloud of comfort.

Someone? Zoe. She was sitting beside the chair, and she had her arm around the little boy Sam recognised as Luke.

Zoe smiled as she saw Sam, and her grip on Luke tightened. Luke's face was bleary with exhaustion and distress, and Sam thought, He's only eight years old, he shouldn't be facing this.

'I tried to get Lorna to take Luke home,' Zoe said softly. 'But she won't. Everyone's so worried about Ryan that maybe…they can't see there's another need. Luckily our ward's quiet so I've had a little time to stay with Luke. He's been telling me all about things to do here. He says Sea World's awesome. I've been thinking I should go.'

Lorna woke up then, and demanded answers. Sam sat and explained things to all of them—that Ryan's heart was failing to such an extent that a transplant was the only option, that Gold Coast City didn't have the facilities to perform transplants, so he'd be moved the next day to start the process of assessment, and his parents would go with him.

'Is he going to die?' Luke whispered, and Sam sent an urgent mental signal to his grandma to reach out and hug him, but Lorna started to cry so it was Zoe who did the hugging.

'Why has Grandma been crying and crying?' Luke asked in a scared whisper.

'Hey,' Zoe said, still hugging. 'No drama. I'm sure your grandma's crying because she's relieved. Ryan might need to wait a while until he gets a donor heart, but once that happens he'll be brilliant. Back to the old Ryan.'

'But transplants don't work,' Lorna sobbed. 'Or if they do they only last a few months.'

Luke's face bleached white—and Sam saw the moment when Zoe decided to stop being gentle and tell it like it was.

'That's nonsense,' she snapped. 'I'm sorry, Lorna, but your information's way out of date. Look at me.'

'You?'

'Me,' Zoe said, and lifted the hem of her baggy uniform tunic and the soft T-shirt underneath. She turned side on so they could all see the long, distorted scar that spelled renal transplant.

'I was the same as Ryan,' she told them. 'I had an infection as a kid, only instead of messing with my heart it messed with my kidneys so I needed a transplant. I was given a new kidney three years ago, and it's working fine. My doctors tell me I'm going to live for ever and I'm even learning to surf. I have so many plans now—plans for the rest of my life. Who says transplants always fail?'

And Lorna's sobs stopped, just like that, and she stared at Zoe as if she was some sort of mirage.

Zoe stayed with her shirt pulled up, as if she knew they needed time to examine the scar.

'Wow,' Luke breathed, and put out a finger to touch it. 'Did it hurt?'

'Nah,' Zoe said with insouciance. 'I'm brave. Isn't that right, Mr Webster?'

'She's so brave she surfs in four feet of water, on eighteen inch waves,' Sam said, and the tension was broken. Even Lorna was smiling as Zoe pulled her shirt back down and got to her feet.

'I need to get back to the ward,' she told them, but then she hesitated. 'Lorna, you said Luke's staying with you. Will he keep staying with you while his parents are with Ryan?'

'Yes,' Lorna said, and Sam watched Luke's face tighten. He could guess what sort of strains this small boy was facing—he'd seen those pressures a lot in the siblings of dangerously-ill children. All attention had been on Ryan for months. Luke would be fitted in around the edges, and now he was being asked to stay indefinitely with an elderly grandmother who looked like she wept more than she kept a child entertained.

'Will you take me to Sea World on Sunday, then?' Zoe asked, and he blinked. What?

'Will *I* take you?' the little boy said cautiously, and Zoe looked a question at Lorna.

'If it's okay with your grandma. Luke, you've lived on the Gold Coast all your life, but I've never been here before. I need a guide—someone to tell me what to see and the cool rides to go on. Is there a Ferris wheel? I love Ferris wheels.'

'But you'll miss your surfing lesson,' Sam said before he could help himself, and copped a reproving look from Zoe for his pains.

'Some things are more important than surfing lessons. I'm on night duty this week, which means I need to sleep on Saturday, so Sunday's the only time I have free. I'm dying to go. Will you take me, Luke?'

'Yes,' Luke said. 'There are cool rides. The Ferris wheel's not at Sea World, though, but there's one near it.'

'Excellent,' Zoe said, and beamed.

'That would be lovely,' Lorna said, and Sam looked at Zoe and thought...*lovely?*

He knew how much she loved surfing. He knew how much she was aching for next Sunday to come. He'd only offered two hours every Sunday, and he knew she'd love more, yet here she was, putting it aside to take a child to an amusement park, to give some fun to a kid who was desperate for time out.

She'd pulled up her top and shown her renal scar and he knew how much she hated doing that, and now she was giving up her Sunday...

'Can I come, too?' he asked, before he even realised he was about to offer, and he found everyone looking at him.

'You?' Zoe said in astonishment.

'They have great water slides,' he said weakly. 'Almost as good as surfing. And I like Ferris wheels. Callie will look after Bonnie.'

'Cool,' Luke said cautiously, and Lorna pulled herself together, thanked them, set a time for them to pick Luke up, and the thing was done. Grandma and grandchild left, and Sam was left in the empty waiting room with Zoe.

'Thank you,' she said, and it needed only that. It was Zoe who was generous. He'd grudgingly given her two hours' surfing a week, and she gave so much more.

'For offering to have fun on Sunday?'

'You like your own company. It'll be more than two hours.'

'Yeah, but I don't have to talk to you all the time,' he told her, and she smiled, and then her smile faded.

'What are Ryan's chances?'

'Good, as long as a transplant's found soon. Thank you for showing your scar. You realise Lorna will tell Ryan's parents and you've just reassured everyone in a way no one else could.'

'My pleasure.'

'It's not your pleasure. You don't like telling people.'

'It's different,' she said. 'I choose to no longer be a renal transplant patient. I choose also to use my experience to reassure others that there is life on the other side.'

'So I can use you for show and tell whenever I need you?'

'I say who, I say when,' she retorted, and he grinned. And then he couldn't help himself, he had to reach out and touch her.

He touched her face, just touched. There was no way in the world he should touch this woman, and yet how could he not? She stood there in her plain hospital greens, she looked tired and a little bit worried, she still had hours of her shift to go, and he was a consultant cardiologist and he had no business at all touching a nurse.

But this wasn't just a nurse. This was Zoe.

Her skin was amazing. Soft, clear, almost luminescent. Her gorgeous, clear eyes were looking up at him, asking a question.

He wasn't sure what the question was.

Or actually…

He did know.

Are you going to kiss me? That's what her eyes were asking, and that's exactly what he did.

And the kiss was like quicksilver. Light, hot, fast… As fast as the feeling that burned right through him as his mouth claimed hers.

She was yielding to him. Her lips were parting. She was leaning forward so he could kiss her…as he wanted to kiss her.

He wanted to kiss her. Every sense in his body wanted to kiss her. She was soft and warm and yielding, and brave and true and gorgeous.

He'd sworn never to touch another woman. He'd sworn never to fall…

That had been before he'd met Zoe, he thought in the tiny section of his brain that was still capable of holding thought. That part was getting smaller by the moment.

He was entirely centred, entirely focussed, on kissing Zoe.

He was holding her, tugging her into him, and she was rising on her toes to come closer. Her arms were around him, and he felt her heat, felt a response from her body that made him tug her closer still.

He was plundering her mouth, tasting her, wanting her, and nothing was more important, nothing could get in the way of here, now, this woman.

Except there was a nurse at the door who was coughing politely, and then coughing a little louder, and trying to hide a grin a mile wide.

'Um, Zoe, we need to do medication rounds,' she said as they broke apart in confusion. 'I'd give 'em myself but hospital protocol says double-check unless it's a Code Blue emergency or State of General Chaos, and I can't quite see what you two are doing as fitting either category.'

And Zoe blushed, adorably, seemingly from the toes up. But then, instead of looking disconcerted or nonplussed or anything he might have expected, she chuckled.

'I was having trouble breathing,' she said. 'Does that count as Code Blue?'

'You want oxygen?' the other nurse said, grinning back, and the situation eased from the potential to be mortifying to something that was…fun? 'Shall I hit the bells? I can have a crash cart here in seconds. Paddles to restart the heart? A bit of defibrillation?'

'I think,' Zoe said serenely, still grinning at Sam, 'that there's quite enough electricity in here already. Thank you, Dr Webster, for what was a very nice kiss. I'm looking forward to going on the roller-coaster with you on Sunday—it should be a wild ride.'

And she swept out with her nursing colleague, and Sam heard them chuckling again as they headed back to the wards and he thought...

He thought maybe he was taking this far too seriously.

He hadn't wanted to kiss her. He hadn't wanted to take this anywhere at all, but Zoe's attitude said it was fine.

Kiss and move on. Have fun.

Fun... The concept was so far from his mindset...

And that was his problem, he thought. Emily's death had darkened his life. He'd been protecting himself ever since.

Zoe was a girl who'd had a transplant, a girl who simply wanted to embrace life.

She'd kissed him, she'd made him feel...like his life could change, and then she'd chuckled and walked away.

And maybe his life had changed.

He looked after her, at the empty corridor, at the echoes of her smile, her chuckle, the remembrance of her kiss, and he thought...

Fun.

Zoe.

He grinned.

Life was okay. He had his Bonnie. He had the best job in the world.

He was taking Zoe to Sea World on Sunday.

He headed back towards his apartment and met two colleagues on the way, both of whom beamed and made it totally clear the whole hospital knew what had just happened in the cardiac care waiting room.

Did he care? No. He was going to Sea World with Zoe.

* * *

Zoe had a very interesting week. She was now officially classified as Gold Coast Central's Hottest Gossip Item, and if she was honest with herself, she was enjoying herself very much indeed.

Somewhere Zoe had read that the happiest people were those who had the most *I'm a*. I'm a daughter, I'm a mother, a teacher, a knitter, a rock climber, a surfer. But for years Zoe's *I'm a* had been confined. I'm a daughter, I'm a renal patient, I'm a cosseted girlfriend.

Now…I'm a nurse and I'm a learner-surfer and I'm Bonnie's daytime carer, and I'm half the equation in sizzling gossip that's zooming around the hospital like wildfire, she told herself, and she liked it.

It was such a weird sensation. She was being seen as…sexy? Dean had never seen her as sexy, she thought, and neither had anyone else in her circle of friends back home. How could she be sexy? She'd been poor Zoe, who needed to be treated with care and kindness, but now… Sexy was delicious.

It wouldn't last. She knew enough about hospital gossip to know it'd die down as something else took over. She and Sam would take Luke to Sea World then they'd resume their weekly surfing lessons. She wouldn't need to care for Bonnie—the fast-recovering dog hardly needed company any more anyway—and the universe would right itself.

She wanted to tell Sam to relax, chill, let it die in its own time, but he was avoiding her. They were having very brief exchanges when they met on the ward. She wanted to tell him that that made it worse—the fact that when he came into her ward he was curt with her rather than his normal friendly self. It raised eyebrows even more.

He was…embarrassed? Mortified?

Well, he'd kissed her, she told herself, so it was his problem. She wasn't about to join him in the mortification department.

It had been a gorgeous kiss. It had made her feel like she'd never felt like in her life and it had added a fabulous *I'm a* to her repertoire.

I'm a hottie.

Sunday.

They were collecting Luke from his grandmother's at ten.

Sam was awake at six, staring at the ceiling.

For once he had no patients in the wards—a situation that happened only a couple of times a year. He had no rounds to do. He could sleep in—or not.

Bonnie was sleeping soundly in her basket beside his bed. She'd taken to being an invalid with aplomb, even seeming to enjoy the extra fuss made of her. He'd had no fewer than three offers to look after her today while he and Zoe went to Sea World.

At ten.

He had four hours before ten.

He had time to go surfing, he decided. He had time to clear his head, to get back to being a loner for a while.

He tossed back the covers and Bonnie opened one eye and looked at him almost indulgently. Two weeks ago she'd have been hammering on the door to go with him, but she was a sensible dog and there were compensations to having a broken leg.

Compensations like spending time with Zoe?

See, that's why he needed to surf. He needed to get his head in order before he spent the day with her.

He took Bonnie out for a quick dose of grass then settled her back to bed. He grabbed a muesli bar and a drink and headed to his car.

And stopped. His conscience was like an elastic band, stretched tight, and it wouldn't let him get to the car.

Zoe was missing her surfing lesson today.

Zoe had volunteered to miss her surfing lesson, he told himself. It had been her decision to forgo her lesson to take Luke to Sea World.

She was giving up her surfing lesson to make a desolate kid happy.

Consciences should be abolished, he told himself savagely, but his feet turned all by themselves and the next minute he was knocking on Zoe's door.

He knocked softly, so as not to wake her if she was asleep, but no such luck. She answered, wearing a gorgeous, pink silk nightie, her curls tumbled, her eyes still drowsy with sleep, but when she saw him she lit up and her smile did things to him...

Things that said back off, run—but it was too late. He'd knocked and she was smiling at him, bright with expectation, and he had no choice but to follow through where his inconvenient conscience had led him.

'You're missing your surfing lesson today,' he said, a bit too gruffly. 'I thought...I'm going surfing now. If you'd like to come...'

'Could I?' Her smile lit up her face. 'Oh, Sam, that's so kind. Can you wait two minutes? I have toast in the toaster. Do you like home-made marmalade? My mum's just sent me some.'

So thirty seconds later he was sitting at her kitchen table, scoffing toast and marmalade, while Zoe dressed and chatted and scooted back and forth to eat her own toast while she got ready, and he felt so domestic, so enveloped in something he could hardly describe…

'So where's Bonnie?' she demanded. She finished off the last piece of toast and licked a trace of butter from her fingers and he thought…he thought…

Where's Bonnie?

'Still asleep,' he managed. 'I took her outside for a few moments so she's comfortable. She'll sleep until we get back, then Callie will look after her while we're at Sea World.'

'She has so many friends,' Zoe said, satisfied. 'Do you want to see the beach gear I've organised for when she's well enough for the beach again?' Without waiting for an answer, she hauled open a cupboard and produced a foldable trampoline-type pet bed, and six slender prayer flags. They were multicoloured, light and easy to set up and they'd be visible for miles.

'I know it's more stuff to carry down the beach,' Zoe said happily, 'but Bonnie and I have been practising. She already likes the bed and she knows to stay when you tell her. And see these little hooks? I've made a canopy—it doesn't work when it's windy but on hot, still days it makes the prayer flags into a shade tent. How cool's that?'

'Really cool,' he said faintly.

'I'm not interfering, am I?' she asked anxiously. 'You don't have to use them, but I thought…it'll keep her safe and let you keep doing what you both love.'

It would.

And then he thought…

It'll keep her safe and let you keep doing what you love…

And with that thought came a blast of longing so powerful he had to close his eyes.

To be able to love this woman…and keep her safe…

'Right,' she said. 'Unless you want more toast, are you ready to go?'

'I'm ready,' he said, but he thought, *Am I?*

The beach was amazing. There were half a dozen serious surfers far out, but no one else was on the beach and the surf was magic. The waves were low, even rolls that started way out but somehow kept their momentum so they were still rideable almost to the shore.

'I'll practise in the shallows. You go out with the big boys,' Zoe said, and normally Sam would, paddling out to where the surf promised to be magic.

This morning it promised to be magic right in close.

Zoe was improving by the minute. He'd never seen such intensity in a novice surfer. She was wobbling to her feet consistently now, managing to balance for a few short seconds, managing to ride the wave a few feet, feeling its power, and every time she did she whooped with joy. Then as the wave finally shook her free she tumbled in freefall, went under and surfaced spluttering, laughing and desperate for more.

She was starting to shake him off now, trying to cope alone.

'I can do it. I'm sure I can. Don't push the board, I can get it. Ohhhh…'

And down she went again, and under, and he reached down and gripped her hands and pulled her up. She surfaced half choking, half convulsed with laughter, and it was all he could do to let go of her hands and obey orders.

To give her space.

He started riding the small waves as well, and a couple of times she caught the same wave and they rose together. Her whoop when they managed it could be heard from one end of the beach to the other. One of the surfers from far out rode a wave all the way in, obviously intending to pack up and leave, but he stopped to watch Zoe for a while and the look he cast Sam left Sam in no doubt as to the guy's jealousy.

'She almost makes me want to turn teacher,' the guy shouted to him as he headed past. 'If nippers were all like this, I'd have stayed in the baby class.'

He gave Sam a good-natured grin, watched a bit more as Zoe wobbled gamely to the shore and then left them.

Sam felt pretty much unbearably smug.

'I must be doing well,' Zoe declared, dragging her board out to the next wave. 'Even my instructor's grinning.'

'You have a long way to go,' Sam said, and Zoe's grin matched his.

'I know I have, and you have no idea how good that feels.'

He thought of the kidney transplant.

He watched her some more and he thought this woman had lived in the shadow of an early death since childhood. Now she had a future and she was embracing it with everything she had.

And Sam...the future...

For some reason, here, now, the loneliness and desolation and self-blame he'd felt since Emily had died were somehow slipping away.

Zoe had had her life restored to her and was making use of it. She was giving him a lesson in living.

As a cardiologist he saw patients on the cusp of death every day, he thought, but he'd never learned this lesson from them.

Zoe was…different.
Zoe was Zoe.

They showered and dressed in the amenity block
above the beach and then had a very satisfactory second breakfast—egg and bacon burgers from the burger
cart above the beach, eaten while fending off a hundred odd seagulls waiting for every crumb.

The sun was warm on their faces. The day was
still ahead of them. Zoe was breaking bits off her
hamburger bun, trying to aim crumbs directly at a
gull with a missing leg. She worked at it, worked at
it, worked at it—and finally her crust landed exactly
where she wanted. Her one-legged gull grabbed it and
flew off—and lowered its 'missing leg' as it flew.

'What a con.' Zoe burst out laughing. 'Of all the
actors…'

He looked at her and he wanted…

He wanted.

'So what do you want to do next?' Zoe asked.

'Go and collect Luke?' he said cautiously, and she
grinned.

'That's not what I mean. I mean…' She gestured
to the sea, to the gulls, to the surfers way out. 'This
is one of my dreams. I have so many I doubt I'll cram
them all in.'

'Like what?'

'Like going to Nepal. Like learning how to make
mango ice cream. Like learning how to jive. I spent so
many years not permitted to do anything that my list's
a mile long. Even mango ice cream… My mother
was paranoid about tropical fruit after I copped an
infection from eating paw paw. My restrictions were

weird, so my list's enormous. What's number one on yours?'

Sitting here, he thought. Eating hamburgers with you.

What else? When he thought about it there wasn't much else. Since Emily's death he'd pretty much concentrated on taking one step after the next.

He'd had lists, he thought. It was as if he was the opposite of Zoe. After Emily's death, his dreams had pretty much ended.

'Save a few more kids,' he said, and she nodded.

'I'll drink to that,' she said, and raised her juice. 'But there must be more. Would you like to…I don't know…learn to propagate man-eating plants? Did you know the *Nepthenthes rajah* can already trap small mammals? I reckon if you tried hard enough you could grow one big enough to trap a tax inspector. I can't fit that into my life plan right now but you could fit it into yours. You might want to be careful of Bonnie, though.'

'Why would I breed carnivorous plants?' he asked.

'Because you've never done it before. Isn't that a good enough reason? Or you could learn to knit hot-water-bottle covers. That'd sit well as an alternate hobby when the surf's lousy.'

'When the surf's lousy I do more work.'

'Because you can't forget Emily's death unless you're either surfing or working?' she ventured.

He stilled. No one had ever been so blunt—but Zoe wasn't even looking repentant.

'Sorry,' she said, still sounding upbeat. 'It's just… I've learned the hard way to say it like it is. I've spent half my life with people tiptoeing round the fact that I might die, so I guess I'm over the niceties. I still might die,' she said, looking surfwards again with satisfaction. 'But I plan to go down doing something on my list.'

'You're planning on dying surfing?' He could hardly say it.

'Are you kidding?' She was scornful. 'Surfing's right at the top of my list. I'm talking about getting way down the bottom. The way I see it, I have years of following dreams. Seventy years if I'm lucky. But you...how can you only have two things?'

'It's the way I like it.'

'Is it?' She rose and tossed the last of her hamburger crumbs to the frenzied mob. 'It seems to me...' She stopped then and seemed to collect herself. 'No. Sorry. It's none of my business. It's just, I've shaken off all my shackles right now and I'm so happy I'd like to see the rest of the world shake theirs off, too.'

'I don't have shackles.'

'Don't you?' she asked, suddenly gentling. 'I think you do but, as I said, it's none of my business. Now, let's go and get Luke.'

They headed back to the Jeep, and as he drove Zoe fell silent. Sam was free to think.

Did he have shackles, self-imposed or not?

If he did then he liked them, he thought. He'd imposed them himself. They weren't shackles so much as a set of rules to keep his world steady.

He wasn't a man to follow his dreams. He'd achieved what he wanted to achieve and nothing else mattered.

Nothing else was permitted to matter.

Bonnie mattered. That moment when he'd thought she'd died... It hadn't been as bad as seeing the wave hurl Emily to the sandbank but it was still bad.

He didn't want to go there again, and if shackles stopped it happening then that was the way he liked it.

He cast a sideways glance at the girl sitting beside him.

Shackles. He needed them, he thought, to keep himself isolated. Isolation was his plan for the future and he didn't intend to deviate.

Shackles?

How strong could he make them?

They collected a very excited Luke and from there there was little time for introspection, or if there was, Zoe and Luke weren't interested.

Sea World. Fishes, dolphins, manta rays and penguins. Rides, rides and more rides. Luke turned into a little boy again, whooping, being loud as Sam suspected he hadn't been loud for a long time, pleading with them to go on the wildest, splashiest ride and crowing in delight when his grown-ups got satisfactorily wet.

Luke and Zoe fed the manta rays, boggled that such huge flappy creatures could have faces that they decreed were almost adorable. They checked out the penguins and practised their waddles and giggled. They stood waist deep in the dolphin pool, and Luke patted the belly of a dolphin called Nudge, who'd been stranded as a baby at sea and had figured by now that humans were trusted friends.

Luke stroked and stroked and maybe the dolphin—or Nudge's handler, who was empathetic and kind—realised this was what Luke needed most in the world, for there was no hurry. Luke was allowed to be a child again for as long as he wanted to be. Zoe stroked too, but mostly she watched Luke, her eyes suspiciously misty.

And despite the vows he'd just reaffirmed for himself, Sam watched Zoe putting herself out there to make sure Luke had the time of his life. He watched her taking every ounce of enjoyment she could wring from the day as well.

He thought…

He had to stop thinking.

'But we still need a Ferris-wheel ride,' Zoe decreed, as Sam checked his watch and finally decided it was almost time to get Luke back to his grandma.

'Do you know where a Ferris wheel is?' A middle-aged woman and her husband had been standing beside them, dolphin watching. Sam had noticed this pair throughout the day and had become a bit concerned. The woman was determined to go on every ride, but her husband had been wheezing along behind her, looking exhausted.

'We've both got flu,' the woman had said when Sam had helped the guy from the last ride, and she'd coughed to prove it. 'But we're from Perth and this our last day here. I want to do everything. But like you, young lady,' she said now, 'I want a Ferris wheel.'

'There's one on the beach,' Luke volunteered. 'There's one really big one but it's ages away and the carriages are all closed in. This one's part of a circus and it's open and looks awesome.'

He must have seen it as his parents drove back and forth to the hospital, Sam thought. A Ferris wheel would seem magic for a kid whose family was solely concerned with keeping his big brother alive.

'Let's go, then,' Zoe declared. 'And then our day has to end.'

'Rats,' Luke said, and Sam thought that was his sentiment exactly.

CHAPTER SIX

THEY DROVE TO the Ferris wheel, and Reg and Marjory, their new friends from Perth, came along as well.

'It'll be a lovely way to finish our holiday,' Marjory said, still coughing. 'Riding up and down, looking out over the mountains and the sea. Won't it, Reg?'

'I guess,' Reg said, but Sam looked at him, looked at his colour and stepped in.

'I reckon you'd be better sitting it out, mate,' he told him. 'You look exhausted.'

'He's not exhausted,' Marjory said, indignant. 'It's our last excitement. Your little boy looks tired, too, and he's not giving up.'

Luke did look tired. He'd pushed himself past his limit. Sam and Zoe had had to split up, doing every second ride to keep up with him, but the difference between Luke and Reg was that Luke looked gloriously happy. Reg just looked spent.

But then Sam got distracted. 'Luke's not our little boy,' Zoe was telling Marjory, and Sam heard an unmistakeable note of regret in her voice.

Whoa. Regret?

Family. Was that on her list?

He looked down at Luke and saw he'd tucked his hand into Zoe's. He was a tired kid at the end of a very long day. He'd go home to his grandma and be faced with all the tensions he'd been facing for months, but for now he was one happy little boy. Zoe was holding him and it felt…it felt…

Okay, it felt like family.

And the faint, insidious questioning became louder.

'Tickets,' Zoe said, and he blinked and realised he was staring at nothing. Reg and Marjory were already lining up to get into their gondola and he hadn't even bought tickets yet.

'Earth to Sam,' Zoe said, and he hauled himself together and they went and bought tickets for one last ride.

It was the end of a glorious day and it was surely okay for a girl to dream.

Zoe had come to the Gold Coast to escape caring. She loved her family to bits, she'd even loved Dean, but they were like the wetsuits Sam wore, keeping the cold at bay but too tight for comfort. She'd been in a cocoon of protection ever since she'd become ill and it was time now to shake it off. In the end she'd had no qualms telling Dean it was over, because she'd realised that all Dean saw in her was someone he could protect. Surely he could use some excitement too, she'd thought, for that was what she wanted. Sizzle.

Sizzle was here, now. The way she was feeling…

She had no business sizzling, she told herself. She had no business sitting on the opposite side of the gondola, looking at Sam Webster, thinking he made her toes curl. Thinking she might even be making his toes curl.

Or was she? Was it her imagination? Wishful thinking?

It wasn't. The way he'd been looking at her all day... the way he'd reacted when her body had touched his...

She needed to take a cold shower, she told herself. Surely it was her imagination. She needed to calm down.

But she didn't want to calm down. She'd left Adelaide looking for sizzle, and sizzle was right in front of her. And if he was interested...

She'd be really interested right back, she decided. She felt a warm, zippy tingle from her toes to her ears and back again, and she wiggled in her safety harness and hugged Luke because a girl had to hug someone and it was far safer to hug Luke than it was to launch herself across the gondola at the man looking at her with hunger...

She was sure it was hunger.

Life was pretty exciting, she decided. This was a truly excellent place to be. The sea and the mountains looked almost dreamlike, the man on the opposite seat looked even more dreamlike—and Zoe Payne thought she might, she just might let herself think about falling in love.

It was a terrifying prospect, but Sam Webster, paediatric cardiologist, surfer, all-round loner, might just not be able to keep those shackles in place.

It was lust, he decided as the Ferris wheel gondola rose ponderously up to the peak, hovered for them to enjoy the view and then started its descent again. It was a mighty fine view, he conceded, but the view in front of him was better.

Somehow Zoe Payne had wriggled under his defences.

Somehow Zoe Payne made him doubt his own plan for isolation.

She was saying something to Luke, something that made the little boy giggle. She glanced up and caught his gaze...and blushed.

She was adorable.

'Do I have fairy floss on my nose?' she demanded, a little bit breathlessly. 'Luke, Sam's staring at me. Do I have fairy floss on my nose?'

'Just freckles,' Luke said. 'He's staring at you 'cos you're pretty.'

'Really?' Zoe demanded, looking immeasurably pleased. 'You think I'm pretty? Wow.' She grinned and hugged him. 'Do you have a girlfriend?'

'No,' Luke said. 'That's silly. You can be Dr Webster's girlfriend, though.'

'He already has Bonnie. Have you met our Bonnie?'

'She visited Ryan when he came into hospital the first time,' Luke told her. 'She's nice, but she's not as nice as you.'

And that was a hard call, Sam thought as the Ferris wheel started to rise again. Who was nicest? His dog or Zoe?

The heart expands to fit all comers. He'd read that somewhere and he hadn't believed it, but now...

Now, though, a tiny niggle was building to a huge doubt. How could he resist?

And then a scream ripped apart the peace of the late afternoon and he needed to turn his thoughts in another direction entirely.

'Sit down, madam, sit down *now*.'

The voice through the megaphone boomed out as the Ferris wheel came to an abrupt, shuddering halt.

Sit down?

They were all sitting. They were harnessed, belted in by the operator with instructions not to undo the harness under any circumstances.

Then came another scream, from a gondola above them.

'He's dead. He's not breathing. Do something. Reg...Reg... Get us down!'

Marjory.

It was the end of a glorious beach day. People were packing up and going home. The Ferris wheel was therefore almost empty. Reg and Marjory were right up the top, two gondolas away from theirs.

Marjory had undone her harness. She was leaning right out of the gondola, screaming hysterically to anyone below.

'Get us down. He's not breathing. Get us down.'

Any minute now she'd fall out, Sam thought incredulously. If the operator started the wheel again she could hit a strut and be knocked out.

'Sit down and do up your harness,' the voice boomed. 'The wheel can't move until you're sitting.'

But Marjory wasn't listening. She was lurching from one side of the gondola to the other, leaning right out as if she could grab someone from below to help her.

'Marjory, sit down,' Sam roared upwards at her, putting every ounce of command he could muster into his voice. 'We can't help you until you sit.'

'He's dying. He's dead.' It was an agonised wail of terror, and Sam realised she wasn't hearing a thing.

'A heart attack?' Zoe whispered, holding Luke close, and Sam looked at both of them and then looked up at the hysterical woman, his mind racing.

Reg had looked to be in his mid-fifties. He was a bit overweight. He'd had flu.

He'd looked…he'd looked like Sam should have intervened, only he'd been distracted by Zoe.

The wheel had come to a dead stop now. Nothing was happening.

'Nothing's moving until you're in your harness,' the voice boomed through the loudspeaker, and Sam looked up at the hysterical Marjory and thought there was no chance of any harness going on.

He unclipped his own.

'Take care of Luke,' he said, tight and hard, and he swung himself up, out and on top of his gondola before Zoe could react.

'Sam!' She didn't scream. She stayed still, she stayed holding Luke, but her face lost its colour.

'I was a monkey in another life,' he said, smiling down at her. 'The light cables make it safe. Luke, hold onto Zoe. She's a bit scared, but you know that this is just like climbing the jungle gym at school. See you soon.'

And he reached up, looped the light cable around his wrist and grabbed the next strut, then swung himself high, grabbed the gondola above, swung, steadied, and heaved himself higher.

Dear God…

He made it look almost easy, Zoe thought as Sam swung himself up through the next gondola and reached for the strut to swing himself to the next one.

It wasn't easy. She couldn't have done it even if it had been at ground level. As it was… How high were they? She wasn't looking down.

She clutched Luke and Luke clutched back.

'Sit down!' The voice below was a continuous roar of instructions but the voice below was as helpless as she was.

Above, Marjory was sobbing, out of control, but Sam was steadily growing nearer. From the other gondolas people watched with horror.

'He's clever,' Luke said, in a far steadier voice than Zoe was capable of. 'My dad said he saved Ryan's life that first night he got sick. He's saving people again.'

He'd reached Marjory. He hauled himself up, swung himself into the gondola and for one appalling moment Zoe thought Marjory would launch herself at him and hug him so hard she'd propel them both out.

But it was Sam who propelled Marjory. He grabbed both her shoulders forced her to sit, and forced her to stay sitting.

'You sit down and you don't move or I won't look at Reg,' he growled, and it was a measure of the terror all around them that silence let Zoe hear every word. 'Sit. Stay.'

And finally, amazingly, Marjory subsided.

So did Sam. He dropped to his knees, obviously to treat Reg, and was lost to sight.

There was a long moment, or more than a moment—who could tell how long?—while Zoe forgot to breathe. She was clutching Luke's hand so hard he yelped and she had to give him a shamefaced smile and release the tension. Just a little bit.

Then…

'We're secure. Bring it down,' Sam yelled, still unseen, but there was no mistaking he was yelling to the operator below and there was no mistaking the authority in his voice.

'Are you in harness?' the guy below yelled, and Sam told him where he could put his harness.

'Move it. Now. I take full responsibility. Just do it,' he yelled back, and finally the gondolas jerked and the wheel came to life and they headed towards the ground.

'Luke, I'll need to help Sam when we get to the ground,' Zoe told the little boy by her side. She still couldn't see what was happening—Sam was still working on the gondola floor—but she was making the same assumption that had made Sam risk his life by clambering up through the struts fifty feet above the ground. Cardiac arrest.

'I know that,' Luke said. 'You're a nurse and Sam's a doctor. I'll be good.'

'You're always good,' Zoe said to him. 'One day soon I reckon we need to organise you to be very, very bad. How about going to dodgem cars next Sunday and seeing how many cars we can crash?'

'Really?'

'Being good pays off,' Zoe said, and thought Sam hadn't fallen during his crazy climb so someone must have been good.

And if Reg was to live…

Yeah, well, that was to come.

The fairground's ground crew proved extremely competent. Zoe would have thought the obvious thing to do when there was drama in a high gondola was to get it to the ground as fast as possible, but the protocol was obviously geared to make people secure first. While someone was screaming, waving in and out of the gondola, the wheel didn't move, but once Sam had Marjory secure, the wheel rolled straight down, not stopping until Reg and Marjory's gondola was on the loading platform.

Someone else had come running to assist the guy operating the wheel. He helped Sam lift Reg out then helped Marjory out as Sam started work on the seemingly lifeless Reg.

Finally Zoe and Luke's gondola was brought in to ground level as well. The attendant opened the gondola on the far side, away from Sam, but Zoe shook him off.

'I'm a nurse, he's a doctor, we're a team,' she said briefly, and she and Luke were ushered out to the right side.

Marjory was crumpled on the ground, keening.

Luke was clutching Zoe's hand, but he had it figured.

'I'll stay still and be good,' Luke said bravely, and he let her go. Zoe thought, Wow, what a kid, and hugged him. She left him standing by Marjorie and went to see how she could help.

'Has someone called an ambulance?' she demanded.

'Yep,' the attendant told her. 'And Joe's gone to get the first-aid pack.'

She nodded, focussing now on Reg. And on Sam.

Sam had him on his back. Cardiopulmonary resuscitation. Heart massage. He had his hands linked, pushing down with fierce, dogged strength. Fifteen beats, then breathe.

She stooped and knelt beside him. 'I'll breathe,' she said.

'There's no mask.' He was out of breath. He'd climbed, he'd have had to roll Reg, clearing his airway, getting him into position, then getting him out of the gondola, all while trying to breathe and pound.

'Tell that to someone who cares,' Zoe said, and

bent and breathed, long, strong breaths that'd make Reg's lungs expand, while Sam pounded with all the strength he had.

She heard a rib crack.

'Breathe, damn you, breathe,' Sam was saying over and over, but he was talking to Reg and it was now Zoe who was breathing.

He'd seemed nice, Zoe thought. Marjory had been voluble and gushing, but Reg had spoken to them a few times during the day. He'd been kind to Luke, and Zoe thought there were probably kids and maybe even grandkids somewhere. People who wanted this man to live.

Come on, Reg...

'You want a defibrillator?' It was the attendant, standing over them, sounding almost apologetic at interrupting, and Sam kept pounding but glanced up and saw what he was offering.

Yes! A decent, comprehensive first-aid pack complete with the portable defibrillators that were increasingly common at large venues.

And masks.

He handed Zoe the mask, she slid it into place and kept right on breathing while Sam shoved the defibrillator into position.

'Three, two, one...' he said, and she pulled back as the defibrillator did its work, then went back to breathing.

Nothing.

'Three, two, one...'

And this time...

Reg's chest heaved, all by itself. He took a ragged, weak breath but it was definitely a breath, air drawn in all by itself.

'Come on...' Sam muttered. 'Live, damn you.'

Zoe breathed a couple more times, then Sam put his hand on her shoulder and she paused.

'Let him take over.'

Would he?

She'd almost forgotten to breathe herself.

CPR hardly ever worked. She knew that. It was supposedly the medical wonder: get to a heart-attack victim in time, administer CPR and, lo, the victim lived. In reality cardiac arrest was almost always fatal and part of medical training incorporated coping with low expectations—coping with the reality that death wasn't caused by lack of expertise.

They'd done all they could. They needed luck now.

They'd already had it in that one shaky breath. They needed more.

Please...

And they had it. Another breath. Another. Another.

Reg's pallid, grey face received a wash of tepid colour.

Please...

And then, blessedly, here came the cavalry. Ambulance, paramedics, oxygen, adrenalin—all the things to make a slight chance a good one. All the things to make Zoe suddenly redundant.

Sam was still working, in charge, taking total control, but Zoe could back off, slipping out of the medical cluster and backing to where Marjory and Luke huddled, together but not together, seemingly both as terrified as each other.

'He's breathing,' Zoe said to both of them. 'Reg is breathing. Marjory, he's still in danger, but he has a good chance.'

And then, because there was nothing else to do

and woman and child were white-faced and shocked and seemingly without speech, she did the only thing left to her.

She took them both into a group hug and held them hard.

Sam had to go with the ambulance. There was no choice. Reg was drifting back to consciousness. His breathing was almost regular but Sam was under no illusions. The most dangerous time after cardiac arrest was the next minute, and the next minute after that. The block that had caused the arrest would still be there. There was no relaxing until Sam got him into the cardiac care unit with blood thinners on board and he could see what he was dealing with.

'Go,' Zoe said, snagging his car keys. 'I'll take Luke home.'

'But—'

'You're thinking I can't drive it?'

'If you can drive your car, you can drive anything,' he said, and then on impulse he tugged her into his arms and, for no good reason, astonishingly, seemingly to him as well as to her, he gave her a swift, hard kiss, then he lifted Luke and hugged him, too, and that was all he had time for.

Two ambulances had arrived, a standard van and the MICA van, Mobile Intensive Care, so there was room for Sam in Mica, with Marjory following in the standard van. Marjory was still weeping.

'I'll catch up with you at the hospital,' Zoe told her, and suddenly Luke tugged Marjory's cardigan, forcing her to look down at him.

'Dr Webster will make him better,' he said. 'He fixes people. He's ace.'

And Marjory sniffed and sniffed again and managed a watery smile and went to join her husband.

'Sam's really good,' Luke said as Zoe ushered him into Sam's car. 'Isn't he?'

'I… Yes.'

'He says I can call him Sam but I like calling him Dr Webster.' Zoe had thought Luke would be upset, but he was recovering fast, and his thoughts were heading off at a tangent. 'Do you think I could be a doctor when I grow up?'

'I'm sure of it.'

'He climbed the Ferris wheel really fast.'

'I don't think all doctors climb Ferris wheels.'

'No,' Luke said. 'But I will and Dr Webster does, too. He's cool, isn't he?

And Zoe thought back to that hard, fast kiss—she could still feel it—she could still taste it—and she thought, yes.

Yes, he was cool.

Or hot, and getting hotter by the minute.

Reg had a blockage in the coronary artery. He'd need a stent to open the artery permanently and he was on the next morning's surgical list. Even though Sam's specialty was paediatric cardiology, Sam worked steadily, making sure the guy was stable, easing the fear, which was enough almost to cause another attack in and of itself. The jury was still out on the damage stress could do to the heart but Sam had his own opinions and he wasn't about to let any of his heart patients face the night in terror.

Then he needed to cope with Marjory—and four younger Marjories, just landed on the express flight from Perth. Reg had four daughters, aged from twenty-six down. Every one of them was a younger version of their mother and every one of them seemed to need their own personal reassurance that their dad would be okay.

They were terrified, and Sam thought back to Marjory's behaviour at Sea World. Reg was the quiet one in this family, the guy who put himself in the back seat as his wife and daughters took the limelight with their extravagant personalities, he thought—and suddenly they'd realised their quiet mainstay wasn't as rocklike as they'd believed.

Sam allayed their very real terror and he thought as long as he got the stent right, Reg might just get a bit of the attention he deserved from now on. Would he like it?

Love was a weird thing, he mused as he finally left them, and as soon as the lift hit his floor he found his feet turning left instead of right, to Zoe's apartment instead of his.

He knocked and she opened the door and she was in her gorgeous bathrobe again, and he thought…

Actually, he didn't think anything. He couldn't, for Zoe reached up, twined her arms around his neck, tugged him down so his face was right by her face—and there was nothing in the world for a man to do but take her face between his hands and kiss her.

He kissed her as a man coming home.

She was warm and soft and yielding. Her kiss was generous, open, welcoming, and he held her and he felt his world shift.

Shackles falling away?

That's what this felt like. He felt rigid control dropping away, the years of discipline, the years of solitude. This was a release that had seemed impossible but which now seemed totally, inevitably right.

This was two becoming one.

He'd heard that line at a friend's wedding. He'd always been cynical. Even when he and Emily had decided to marry he could hardly remember asking—it had seemed like the sensible, practical thing to do. They had been friends, colleagues and lovers, but there'd been no real connection.

But he hadn't known there'd been no connection because he hadn't felt what that was until now.

So now he held Zoe and he kissed her and he felt like he'd come home. So much for shackles. So much for isolation. They stood in the corridor and nothing mattered except that they hold each other, that he had this woman in his arms and she seemed like she wanted to stay there for ever.

Oh, this kiss... It was something he'd never felt before. The heat from her body...the sweet, aching desire...the need he could feel reciprocated straight back to him.

This woman.

His heart.

How corny was that? He was a cardiologist. The heart was a mass of tissues, muscles, blood vessels. It could even be transplanted. But he wasn't being a cardiologist right now, he thought. He was a man claiming a woman.

Or letting a woman claim him.

'You...you want to come in?' she managed when finally, finally she could get a word out, and he set her back at arm's length and looked at her, really looked at her. He knew what she was asking. He knew what she was offering, and it twisted his heart.

Yeah, that dumb bunch of tissue, muscle, blood vessels was being twisted and it made not the tiniest bit of clinical sense but, dammit, it was twisting anyway and he wasn't asking questions.

'Yes,' he said. 'If you'll have me.'

'Bonnie's on my bed.'

'Bonnie's been an invalid for long enough,' he told her, tugging her close and kissing her hair. 'Medical protocols says urgent cases get the most suitable beds. Are we an urgent case?'

She chuckled, a lovely, low chuckle that made that mass of internal tissue twist all over again.

'Why yes, Dr Webster,' she said demurely. 'Why, yes, I believe we are.'

He woke and there was a woman cocooned against his body. She was curved against him, spooned against his chest. He'd gone to sleep holding her and it seemed that during the night they'd only grown closer.

He'd never felt like this.

Lovemaking with Emily had been good, excellent even, but afterwards she'd always shifted firmly to her side of the bed, setting boundaries. He'd never been able to cross those boundaries. She'd resented the least interference with her independence, and she'd died because of it.

If he hadn't said the waves were too dangerous, would she have gone out? The question haunted him, because he knew there was a strong possibility that the answer was no.

He hadn't been able to protect her. She'd reacted with fury every time he'd tried to restrain the craziest of her impulses, and tragedy had been the result.

Yet here magically was her antithesis. Here was a

woman who invited him into her bed, who gave herself to him with joyful, laughing abandon, and who in her sleep was giving still.

Zoe.

He held her close, he felt her breath, her chest rising and falling, he felt her warmth and her loveliness, and he felt as if here was a gift without price.

A woman to love.

A woman he could protect and cherish for ever.

She didn't want to wake up.

From the time Zoe had first been diagnosed with kidney disease she'd schooled herself not to want. Not to want the health that other kids took for granted. Not to want their freedom. Not to want their futures.

But now…

Now she had health and freedom and future, and somehow, in the space of a few short weeks, they'd become totally centred on one gorgeous man.

Sam.

He had ghosts, she thought as she lay cocooned against him, savouring the spine-tingling sensation of skin against skin, of the warmth of passion spent, of love.

For it was love. She knew it. Every fibre of her body knew it, but she saw it with clear eyes.

Sam was hero material. He was a gorgeous, sun-bronzed surfer. He was a cardiologist at the top of his game. He was a guy most women would die to get close to—and she'd heard from the hospital gossip that there were many women in this hospital who'd tried.

But he'd lost his Emily, and in a weird way it made him the same as her. Human.

Most medics faced life and death every day but

it still didn't teach them what she'd learned the hard way—that there was no personal promise of life. That your own life could be snatched away. That life was for living, here, now.

Losing your fiancée would do that to you, too, she thought, and maybe it explained this instant connection.

Or maybe nothing explained it. Maybe it was magic, and if it was…she was content to take it.

Just for now?

Maybe not. Lying here in the soft dawn light, with Sam's arms around her, feeling his naked body holding her, she let herself dream.

What if his dreams became her dreams?

This was just the start. All those dreams she'd had while she'd waited for a transplant, while she'd watched from the other side while her friends and family had got on with their lives…

She wanted to do stuff. The first step had been to escape the cloying care of her family, not in a way that would hurt them but in a way that would make it clear she was well and independent and free.

The next step was to earn enough money to travel.

She wanted to climb a Himalaya.

Not a very big one, she conceded. She didn't plan on making climbing her life's work, but already she was researching Nepal and looking at the easier treks and making plans.

She also had other things on her wish list. When she'd talked to Sam about them she'd been deadly serious.

She was learning to surf. She wanted to learn to scuba dive.

She wanted to learn to tango as well as jive.

She felt Sam stir and she wriggled deliciously against him and thought…and thought…

'Can you tango?' she asked.

'Um…right now?' He tugged her close and she smiled and wriggled round so she was facing him.

'I forgot the rose to put between my teeth,' she said. 'But hypothetically…'

'No,' he said.

'Would you be brave enough to learn?'

'I might,' he said, cautious, and she smiled a cat-got-the-cream smile and snuggled closer.

Sam Webster…

He had no ties, she thought. Unlike Dean, who'd wanted to stay in their home town for the rest of their days, paying off their mortgage, tending their garden and raising their two point five children—or actually, no, because he wasn't sure she should have children, there was an increased risk because of the transplant, and she wasn't supposed to dig in the garden because of germs, but if she wore gloves and was very careful…

'Zoe, there's a wedding on this Saturday,' Sam said, and she stilled because her thoughts had been flying ahead, to climbing mountains, ignoring germs, taking risks, all the things she'd dreamed of since her transplant had worked, but now there was this delicious extra dimension, a dimension called Sam…

A wedding this Saturday. Surely it was a bit soon for Sam's thoughts to be going in that direction.

'A wedding,' she said, in the same cautious tone that he'd used when they'd discussed *the tango*. Only possibly more cautious.

'Our nurse manager of Cardiac Care, Alice, is getting married. I'm invited.'

And he said that in the same voice he might have said, 'There's a loaded gun pointed at my head.'

She giggled. She was totally, gloriously happy. Her body was wide awake now and so was his. His hands were starting to do delicious things to her. She felt… sated, she thought, and yet not sated. She wanted more.

'So I need to go,' he said. 'Would you like to come with me?'

'Will there be tango?'

'I wouldn't be surprised.' He was still using the loaded-gun voice.

'Excellent.' There was a couple of minutes' silence after that, a necessary silence because his fingers were doing something to her that took her entire concentration. A girl could explode at the feel of those fingers, she thought. She felt like she could explode. Maybe she already had.

'Wedding?' he said.

'Y-you're catching me at a weak moment.'

'I'm feeling pretty weak myself.'

'You could have fooled me.' She took a couple of deep breaths and forced herself to think. 'Sam, if we go to this wedding…the hospital will—'

'Talk,' he said. 'But do you think every single person from neurologist to ward clerk doesn't already know we're in bed together right this minute? The walls in this hospital have ears, and not only do they have ears, they have great gossipy mouths.' He gathered her further into his arms then rolled and pushed himself up so he was smiling down at her with that gorgeous, wicked grin that made her melt…

But how could she melt? She had already melted.

'Do you mind that they'll talk?' he asked, and she struggled to find the strength to speak.

'How could I mind?' she managed. 'Unless you don't intend to make love to me again, right this minute, and then I mind very much indeed... Oh...'

And then she stopped speaking. She stopped minding. There was nothing in the world but this man. He was the centre of her universe, and Zoe Elizabeth Payne didn't mind anything else at all.

'That was fast.'

He'd taken Bonnie for a brief walk downstairs. Zoe was in the shower. He'd have liked to shower with her—he'd have liked that more than just about anything—but it was Monday morning. Zoe started day shift today, he had patients booked, a ward round to do, things he had to organise for Reg—that stent needed to go in this morning...

How soon before he could take a holiday and spend a couple of weeks making love to Zoe?

'Hey,' Callie said, hauling him back to earth with a jolt as he carried Bonnie down the front steps from the apartment building. Bonnie could walk but stairs were still forbidden. Callie was heading home from the beach. She looked like she'd just been on a beach walk—clean and fresh and windblown. 'I said something,' she retorted.

So she had. He'd been thinking about...other things. He replayed Callie's words in his head, this time focussing. *That was fast.*

'Bonnie's recovery?' he tried, and Callie grinned.

'Nice try, wise guy, but you know very well what I'm talking about. Our Zoe.'

How fast had she become *our Zoe*?

Callie was eyeing him with interest as he set Bonnie onto the grass—but also with a certain degree of scepticism. She was moving into mother-hen mode? With Zoe?

'I'm not messing with your new best nurse,' he growled.

'You'd better not be.'

'So you warned Cade, and now you're warning me?'

'You got it.'

'I'm not messing,' he said, and her eyes widened.

'Really?'

'Really.'

There was a moment's silence and then she reached out and hugged him. 'Oh, Sam, that's awesome. Though…' She hesitated. 'It is pretty fast.'

'Emily and I were together for eight years and we didn't get it right. Maybe fast's the way to go,' Bonnie was sniffing round the grass, taking time to find the perfect spot. Usually Callie greeted Sam with curt friendliness and moved on, but she'd stopped. They were both watching Bonnie, but there were undercurrents.

'So what about you and Cade?' Sam asked, and he was right—there were definitely undercurrents. Callie bristled like a cat who'd just spotted an intruder in her garden.

'What about me and Cade?'

'The grapevine says you're sparking off each other like lightning rods.'

'He's pretty much insufferable.'

'He's a fine doctor.'

'And he's insufferable.' She sighed. 'You realise Alice has invited him to her wedding—and he's accepted. If you take your Zoe…'

His Zoe. Two weeks ago those words would have made him run a mile. Now they had him thinking of what Zoe was doing right now, standing naked in the shower while he stood out here and…

'You are taking her, right?'

'Um…yes.'

'I had you and me as a nice handy pair,' she said, and sighed. 'Now it's you and Zoe, and me and—'

'Cade. Are you going to toss sparks all through the wedding?'

'I'll be good,' Callie said. 'But he really is insufferable. At least you're not any more,' she said as Bonnie finished what she needed to do and limped back to join them. 'Aloof and alone… How insufferable was that? But now our Zoe has made you rejoin the human race, and speaking for the whole hospital we couldn't be more delighted.'

He went surfing that evening and Zoe was there. Zoe and Luke. They were building the world's biggest sandcastle.

Why hadn't she taken Luke to the beach near the hospital? he wondered. But then he thought, no, the Spit was closer to where Luke's grandma lived. Then he thought maybe Zoe had guessed he'd be surfing here tonight. That was a good thought, and then Luke beamed and bounced up to him and there were no regrets at all.

He put his board down as Luke ran to meet him. He picked him up and swung him round and round until the little boy squealed his delight and then demanded to have a turn on the board as well.

'Where's Bonnie?' Zoe asked, standing and brushing sand from her shorts. He looked at her gorgeous, sandy legs. He looked at the huge sandcastle she and Luke had built, and how happy and relaxed Luke was, and the feeling grew in his heart that this was right, the cards had fallen and he had a stack of aces, or maybe just one ace, but if that ace was Zoe then it was fine by him.

'She's in the Jeep.'

'Bring her down on the sand,' she suggested. 'I'll take care of her while you teach Luke to surf.'

He hadn't intended to teach Luke. Three weeks ago he hadn't intended to teach anyone. But Luke and Zoe were both bright-eyed and expectant and he felt more of his armour shift. What armour? he thought hopelessly. It was all gone.

'Don't you want to swim yourself?' he asked, and she shook her head.

'I've done a full day on the wards, we had drama after drama and I'm tired. It'll suit me to lie on the sand with Bonnie and watch my...watch *the* men do manly stuff on surfboards.'

He smiled but instead of picking up her slip of the tongue he was suddenly worried. She did look tired.

'It's not too much for you?' he asked.

'No.'

But his concern was still there. 'Zoe, should you be working full time? If it makes you tired...you might be better doing half-shifts.'

She froze. Something on her face said he'd made a major mistake.

'I've had a big day,' she said, carefully and slowly. 'That's all. Every nurse on our ward was tired today.'

'But—'

'There are no buts.'

'Zoe, it's natural to—'

But her irritation was growing. 'Worry? No, it's not,' she snapped. 'One hint that I'm tired and you're worrying whether I should be working full time?' She took a deep breath. 'This is because of the transplant, isn't it? Don't do that to me, Sam.'

'I didn't.'

'You did. If you hadn't known…'

And she was right, he conceded. Gold Coast City was an acute-care hospital catering for a massive population. There were times when they were run off their feet. He was accustomed to colleagues looking tired.

But Zoe was different.

Because of the transplant?

'Will Ryan still get sick after he gets a transplant?' Luke asked in a small voice, and he hauled himself together, but Zoe got there faster.

'Of course he will,' she said, glaring at Sam like he'd committed murder. 'Just like you get sick. You get colds, you stub your toes on rocks and you fall over and hurt yourself playing footy. Ryan will do those things, too. Right now everyone's being very careful of him, and they'll need to do that until he gets a transplant and for a little while afterwards until he's fully recovered.

'But then he'll be like you and me and all of us. He won't need to be wrapped in cotton wool and he won't have to resign from a full-time job because one day he gets tired. What nonsense. Off you go, the pair of you. Go play in the surf while Bonnie and I have a wee nap because we choose to. Not because we must. Invalids—huh! Off you go, shoo, and don't you dare do that to me again, Sam Webster, ever.'

She lay on the sun-warmed sand with Bonnie and watched Sam teach an eight-year-old to surf.

Luke was a faster learner than she was, but she

wasn't envious. She loved watching them. Sam had Luke waist deep in the waves, lying on the board, pushing it into every likely wave and then whooping with Luke as the little boy managed to wobble to his feet and waver the few feet to the shore.

She'd kind of like to be with them but it was nice to lie here and watch them, too, and hug Bonnie and let herself dream. As she'd been dreaming ever since she'd met Sam.

Only now there was a tiny niggle imposing itself on her dream.

'Zoe, should you be working full time?'

The question had slammed her straight back to Adelaide, straight back to Dean.

Zoe, let me carry that. Zoe, it's too cold for you. Zoe, I don't want you staying up late. This job is far too demanding—remember you have to protect yourself.

Only she hadn't been allowed to protect herself. Dean had done it for her.

If Sam started that nonsense…

He wouldn't.

He might. The way he'd said it…

'If I want to climb Everest, he might try and stop me,' she told Bonnie, and Bonnie looked at her, puzzled.

'Yeah, okay, you have a broken leg and the last thing you want to think about is climbing Everest,' she told Bonnie. 'But how about when your leg is healed and you want to run again, really run, and all your dog friends say, no, don't run because you might hurt your leg again. What's the point of a beautifully-healed leg if you're never allowed to be normal again?'

Bonnie put her big head on her lap and looked dolefully up at her, as if seeing the problem in all its horror. A life without running...

'It won't happen,' Zoe told her, trying to sound sure. Trying to feel sure. 'Sam has too much sense to let it happen. He made one mistake and I've explained and now he won't make it again. He's smart, our Sam. He knows there are invalids and invalids, and we don't fit the job description. We're over it and we want to live.'

He'd overreacted, Sam thought as he held Luke on the board, but so had Zoe. It was okay to worry. It was almost reasonable, especially...the way he was feeling.

If he cared, he'd have to worry. Hell, he'd lost Emily—and he was a cardiologist. He knew bad things happened; he knew how life could turn to death so quickly.

But Zoe wouldn't want that hanging over her for the rest of her life. He could see that.

So...no overt worry. But to ask him not to worry at all...

Care brought worry. He hadn't wanted to care, but caring had been thrust upon him, whether he wanted it or not.

He glanced up the beach to where Zoe was chatting to Bonnie. She *was* tired, he thought, but justifiably. This was still a relatively new job. The kids' ward was hard and he knew today had been frantic, yet she'd contacted Luke's grandma and brought Luke to the beach tonight, pushing herself to make one small boy happy.

And now... She could be lying in the shallows but instead she was intent on making a dog happy.

She was totally, absolutely gorgeous. She was everything he wanted in a woman, and how was a man not to care?

He'd try not to do it overtly, but some things Zoe would need to accept.

She must.

At this time of evening, on a weeknight, this beach was practically deserted, but as Zoe decided maybe she'd best stop watching Sam for a while, stop thinking how drop-dead gorgeous he was and how sexy, she turned her attention to the rest of the beach and realised they weren't the only ones here. A couple of hundred yards along, two kids were digging a hole in the sandy cliff chewed out by the tide. Winter storms had eroded the cliff to form a perilous overhang. There seemed to be some sort of cave behind, and the kids were digging their way in.

Uh-oh. Soft sand. Digging. Even from where she was sitting they made her feel nervous.

Finally she asked Bonnie whether she thought she could manage a short walk. Bonnie thought she could, and they ambled along to see what the kids were doing. They were two almost-grown boys with a project.

A dangerous project.

She edged a bit closer, growing more and more concerned as she realised the level of risk.

'Hi,' she said at last, trying to figure a way to approach this. She'd nursed in paediatrics long enough to known thirteen- or fourteen-year-old kids didn't take kindly to young women telling them what to do, and what authority did she have anyway?

The boys had dug so far in that they were now inside their sandy cave. One stuck his head out and looked at her defiantly.

'Woderyawant?'

Uh-oh. His belligerence was a warning sign all by itself.

'It's a great cave,' she said cautiously. 'But it looks a bit risky. Have you thought about shoring timbers?'

'Wot?'

'Timber supports,' she said. 'All miners use them. Without shoring timbers, these sorts of tunnels cave in all the time. It's a horrible way to die, choking slowly on sand. Yours looks a bit scary. I'd hate you to be buried.'

'This won't fall in,' the kid said scornfully, and Zoe looked at the soft sand and thought maybe diplomacy wasn't the way to go.

'Yes, it will,' she said. 'Soft sand always does.'

'There's tree roots holding it up,' he said belligerently. 'And it goes right in behind the sand. Piss off.'

'The lady's right.'

Zoe had been so intent on the kids and the danger that she hadn't heard Sam come up behind her, but here he was, holding Luke's hand. Both of them were dripping wet. Luke looked excited and interested. Sam looked grim. Had Sam seen where she was going and noticed the risk as well?

Obviously he had.

'Get out,' he said, in a tone that said it was non-negotiable. 'Get out now, or I'll get in there and haul you both out by the scruffs of your dumb necks. This whole thing's about to collapse. Do you want to be buried alive? Out. Now.'

What was it with this guy? If she'd said it they'd have ignored her—she knew it—but there was no way Sam could be ignored. The boys emerged, but they looked sulky and defiant, and she thought, They'll be back. As soon as we're off the beach they'll dig again.

But Sam hadn't finished. He waited until they were clear of the entrance then he bent and checked inside, then leaped lightly up the scarp. There was a dead salt bush right above the boy's cave. That had the roots the boys had been depending on for stability. He grabbed the dead bush by the trunk, hauled and leaned back. The roots came free—and the entire piece of escarpment slid down across the cave entrance.

The *whumph* from the collapsing sand was enough to send a tremor under their feet—and for Zoe to realise how appalling the risk had been.

'Sand goes right into your lungs,' Sam said conversationally. 'You can't stop it. If I catch either of you doing anything so stupid again, I'll get the lifeguards to ban you from the beach all summer.'

'You can't,' one of the boys muttered.

'Try me.'

'It was just a bit of fun,' the other boy said, and Sam relented.

'Yeah, I know, but it was still dumb. I work at the hospital and we see too many kids come in dead. It's not great being dead. I suspect it could be really, really boring. Pack it in, guys.'

They packed it in. The skulked off over the sand hills and Sam and Zoe and Luke were left staring at the collapsed scarp, thinking what could have happened.

Luke bent down to examine the bits of tree trunk in the sand, tugging at a branch that was almost entirely buried.

'They would have died,' the little boy said, horrified, and Sam stooped and lifted him and hugged him.

'Probably not,' he said. 'Probably they would have

been buried up to their armpits in sand and they'd have had to stand here all night feeling sillier and sillier. So I scared them a bit too much. I'm sorry I scared you, too.'

'You scared them to stop them being dead.'

'Yes,' he said.

'It must be awful, being dead,' Luke said in a small voice, and Sam hugged a bit harder, and Zoe knew this had suddenly switched from boys and sandhills to one big brother with a failing heart. 'Is it awful?'

'I don't think it is,' Sam said honestly. 'I know I said it might be boring but that was just to scare them. All I know, Luke, mate, is that I'm a doctor and it's my job to stop people being dead. I try everything I possibly can. To watch these kids take risks…'

'They were having fun,' Luke said.

'Dumb fun.'

'Isn't it okay to have fun?'

'Not if it involves risks,' Sam said flatly, and there was something about the way he said it…there was something there that suddenly made Zoe feel uneasy. The qualms of half an hour ago resurfaced.

She didn't want to take risks, she thought—or not many. Not serious risks. But she did want to have fun.

Twelve months ago, when she'd passed her final nursing exam, she'd sent off for some brochures on climbing in Nepal. She'd shown them to Dean.

'We can do this now,' she'd told him excitedly. 'If we save…there's nothing stopping us.'

'Are you kidding? The risks…'

'There can't be all that much risk. I'm not suggesting Everest. An escorted trek below the snow line…'

'And if you get sick?'

'Then I'll die happy,' she'd retorted, which had been

a dumb thing to say because he really did think she was risking all. The conversation had stopped there and she'd known, right from that moment, that she wouldn't be marrying Dean.

Like she knew, right now, that there could be no future for her with Sam.

He might change, she told herself, but it felt like a forlorn little hope. There was that look on his face that said some things were non-negotiable. A dead fiancée. No risks.

'Zoe? Are you okay?' he asked. Maybe she looked paler than usual. Yeah, okay, the cave incident had scared her but for him to ask that question…the question that had been hanging over her for years…

Zoe? Are you okay?

'I'm fine,' she snapped, and then fought for and found a recovery. 'Sorry, yeah, it must have frightened me a bit, too. They were dopes, Luke.'

'I'll ring the council,' Sam told them. 'The overhang is too large—the storms have really undercut it. They'll get a bobcat along here and knock the top off. Problem solved.'

'Great,' Zoe said, but her 'great' came out flat.

'You didn't really think I should have let them keep digging?' he demanded, incredulous as he heard her intonation, and she shook her head.

'Of course not. Of course you're right, and thank you for sorting it. I just…I just can't help it if I hanker for a tiny bit of risk myself.'

'Not being buried in sand.'

'No, but there are some risks worth taking,' she muttered. 'Not dumb ones, but fabulous ones, and I have my whole life to find out what they are.'

CHAPTER SEVEN

SAM DIDN'T UNDERSTAND and she let it go. Maybe she was wrong, she decided. Maybe she was overreacting. Sam was gorgeous and maybe she was stupid for having any qualms at all.

She took Luke home, returned to the hospital and Sam was waiting. He cooked her steak and chips, and they made toe-curling love and she slept in his arms.

He held her tight, possessively, and the niggle of doubt refused to go away.

She was being dumb, she thought. She was being over-sensitive. What Sam had done with the sand cave had been entirely rational, and his talk about risk had simply been reaction.

Relax, she told herself. You're falling for the most gorgeous guy in the universe, so why not let yourself fall?

It was easy to fall when she was in his arms. She could lie here for ever, she thought... And not take risks?

Bonnie whuffled in her basket at the end of the bed and she thought how domestic this was. How wonderful. Life was so good.

Put the doubts aside and soak in wonderful.

Soak in Sam.

* * *

The hospital had no doubts. Sam and Zoe were now an established item. She copped good-natured teasing from all sides, and she was accepted as an even more deeply ingrained member of the Gold Coast team. She worked through the week in a daze of happiness, with Sam popping in and out of her ward—he did have two kids on the ward as patients so there was no reason at all why every kid in the ward seemed primed to make lovey-dovey teasing noises every time he walked in.

Her colleagues sniggered and Zoe blushed—and tried to put away the tiny niggles that had surfaced and were refusing to be suppressed.

Luckily—or maybe unluckily—she was busy. The weather was vacillating from gorgeous to perfect. This was the middle of the northern-hemisphere summer holidays and the Gold Coast was swarming with tourists who did stupid things.

Things like drowning.

Liam Brennan was eleven years old, here with his family from Ireland. His parents had seen the vast, wide expanse of open beach and had elected to swim not in the patrolled part of the main beach but in a secluded area half a mile from the lifesavers' flags.

His parents couldn't swim. Liam could, a little, but not enough to fight the rip that grabbed him and took him out to sea. A local surfer had come to his aid but not fast enough. He was brought into hospital unconscious, and even though Zoe wasn't one of the medics involved in his treatment, she felt the hush through the department and she knew what the outcome would be.

Resuscitating drowning kids was a miracle but more miracles were needed to stop brain damage caused by interrupted blood supply.

Liam hadn't had that second miracle.

He was on life support, and grief and anger at such needless loss washed through the hospital.

The day after he was brought in, Sam came to find her on the wards.

'I need to speak to you,' he said, and his face was grim. Uh-oh. One look at him and she knew something serious had happened.

'Bonnie?' she said, feeling ill.

'Bonnie's fine,' he said. 'Zoe, I've organised a fill-in for you for a while. Please, we need to talk.'

Bemused, she followed him. She'd thought they'd go into the nurses' station, deserted at the moment, but instead he led her into the lift, down and out to the small garden where he walked Bonnie.

By which time she was starting to feel seriously freaked. What? Images of her parents and siblings flooded into her mind. They'd have contacted her directly if anything dire had happened. Surely?

Or maybe they'd rung the hospital and asked someone close to tell her...

Sam stopped and turned and faced her—and saw her face and swore and grabbed her hands.

'Zoe, no, I didn't mean to scare you. Hell. I didn't think... It's just... I've just come from Liam's bedside—the kid brought in from the near drowning.'

She might have known. He looked sick. Relief on her own account was replaced by sadness for others. *Any man's death diminishes me...* She thought of John Donne's words and she thought how much worse they were when that death was that of a child.

This man spent his life fighting for children's lives. To lose one because of ignorance was particularly gut wrenching. There were signs up all over the Gold

Coast, including in the airport itself. *Swim Between the Flags.* Nearly every drowning here was that of a tourist who thought the gorgeous surf looked harmless. The locals knew the safe places. Tourists had no idea.

'We're about to turn off life support,' Sam said, and he gripped her hands harder.

She held him just as hard and then tugged him close so she was pressed against him.

'I'm so sorry.'

'Aren't we all?' He held her for a long moment, his chin resting on her hair. 'But, Zoe, this isn't about that. I mean…I'm not here for comfort. I've faced kids' deaths before.'

'But not got used to them,' she said, still holding him.

'No.'

She held him for a long, long moment. This was a man who walked alone, she thought, but alone wasn't working. He tried to be dispassionate but it didn't work. A child's death defeated him.

'What?' she said at last. 'Sam, what made you come and organise me to be taken off the ward?'

'I need you.'

'Yeah, of course you do.' She pulled away a little and tried a smile. 'I'm a very useful person. I can see that. But why now?'

'I need you to talk to Liam's parents about organ donation.'

She stilled.

'It's a huge thing to ask,' he said softly into her hair. 'And it's your choice. No one knows I'm asking you to do it. You're free to say no, and there'll be no mention of it ever again. No thought of it. It's just…'

'Just what?' she said in a scared little voice she

couldn't control, a voice that had him pulling away, holding her at arm's length.

'Hell, Zoe, I can't... I'm sorry. Forget I said—'

'Say it,' she said, and she had herself under control again. Sort of.

'Liam's parents are facing withdrawal of life support. I've been with them. They've been approached by the donor organ team. Our counsellor, Sarah, is good. She's incredibly sensitive, no pressure, and she'll back right off if they don't want to go ahead. But Liam's dad wants to donate, very badly. He keeps saying something good has to come out of this mess, and I know, from past experience, that it'll help long term if it does. Only Liam's mum is wavering. Mary keeps saying it'll only drag out other parents' misery. She says transplants fail eventually. She's been watching her son die for two days and all she sees is that transplants make that waiting longer.'

'So you want me...'

'If you could bear it, you could give them a gift,' he said gently. 'The gift of hope, that their son's death could mean the gift of life for someone like you.'

And he said *someone like you* in such a way...

He loved her. She found herself blinking back tears in a sudden rush of emotion that had nothing to do with the death of one little boy but everything to do with the vulnerability of this man before her, and the knowledge that he'd lost and closed himself to the world but now was opening up again.

He was needing her?

It was a heady emotion, and she shouldn't be crying, but there was Liam's death as well, and Emily's death, and suddenly she found herself thinking of the twenty-year-old kid who'd crashed his car the night before her transplant. She shouldn't know the identity of her donor but it was pretty hard not to know.

He'd given her the gift of life. Could she share back?

Life was so precious. Life was standing in the morning sun, with the sea in the background, with this man asking her to share her story.

He was asking her to share more.

There were still doubts—she knew there were—but at this moment there were no doubts at all.

Liam's parents wished for reassurance she could give them. If she could, she'd give them their son's life back, but some things were impossible.

Instead she'd give them what this man asked of her. Faith in hope.

She was perfect.

Sam stood in the background while Zoe talked softly to Liam's parents, showed them her scar, talked them through what had happened to her, talked them through where she was now, her hopes for the future— she even showed them a corny picture she'd made him take with her phone, of her first wobbling stand-up on his surfboard.

'I can do anything I like now,' she told them. 'I have my whole life in front of me but, you know, there's not a day I don't think of the boy who gave me my kidney. The boy whose parents' loss meant my parents didn't have to face that loss. The boy I'll love for ever, because he's part of me.'

'Do you have to be…careful?' Liam's mother whispered, holding Zoe's phone and looking at the blurry photo.

'No,' she said, and suddenly she was almost fierce. 'At least, not any more than I ought to be even if I hadn't had a transplant. Do you have a clear image of Liam on that last day, on the beach?'

'I… Yes,' his mother whispered. 'Of course.'

'And he was happy?'

'Yes,' his dad said, with a fierceness that matched Zoe's. 'He was in heaven. He had the whole beach, sand, sea, sun on his face. He used my phone to send pictures to his mates, boasting of how he was in Australia in the surf. We were mucking round in the waves; he was standing on my shoulders, diving. It was the best…'

'That's what I want,' Zoe said as the big man's face crumpled and as his wife moved to hold him and Sam moved to hold her. 'I want the best. Liam and I…we're going to go out happy.'

'We shouldn't have…' the man said, and Zoe shrugged Sam off and reached and grabbed the guy's shoulders.

'Never say that,' she said. 'It was a freak wave. It could have happened between the flags; it could have happened anywhere. Liam died having the best holiday of his life, and if you decide on organ donation then others will have the best holidays of their lives, too. But right now others don't matter. This is all about Liam, all about you. You talk about it and you make the right decision for you and for Liam.' She hugged them both.

'Sam and I are leaving you now,' she told them. 'This decision is yours, but know that we'll be thinking of you every step of the way, as almost everyone in this hospital is. No blame,' she said again, even more fiercely. 'You do what you need to do for the future. You do what you need to for Liam. You'll know what that is because you love Liam, he's your son, and whatever you decide, whatever the future holds, that love lasts for ever.'

Sam guided her out into the corridor. He closed the door on the grieving parents and then he took her into his arms and kissed her.

It was a long, loving kiss, a kiss of affirmation, of strength, of healing, and when he finally drew away Zoe knew that Sam wanted her as no man had ever wanted her.

He loved her.

And she let herself be loved. The emotion of the last few moments had been heart-wrenching. She let herself lean on his chest, taking strength from him, feeling his heartbeat, feeling…him.

It couldn't last. They were in a main hospital corridor. He was in his gorgeous suit, consulting cardiologist, and she was in her nurse's scrubs.

She needed to blow her nose. Somehow she managed to tug away, to find a tissue and blow, hard.

When she finished he was grinning at her, and a couple of orderlies walked past and grinned, too, and she thought she may as well stand on the rooftop and declare they were engaged.

Engaged? There was a strong word.

Scary? Definitely scary, but the way he was looking at her… Engaged? Definitely possible.

If he asked, would she say yes?

Not yet, she thought, suddenly panicked. There were still doubts. There was still…life.

She thought of Liam's mum's words.

'Do you have to be careful?'

No.

So should she fling herself into Sam's arms and stay there? Surely that wasn't being careful?

He was gorgeous. He was kind and clever and capable. If she took him home, her mum and dad would almost swoon with delight.

They'd think he was safe.

'Dr Webster?' It was Callie; of course it was Callie. The lady was almost a part of the walls in this hospital—or maybe it was just that she was a friend and Zoe was aware that she cared for her and was watching with interest to see what would happen.

'Sarah's reporting that Liam's parents want to go ahead with organ donation,' she said. 'Sam, they'd like you with them when they turn off life support.'

'I'll come,' Sam said.

'And they said to tell you thank you,' Callie said, eyeing Zoe warmly. 'Zoe, only Sam and I know what you just did, but we thank you, too. I guess…Sam has just been thanking you personally?'

'I… Yes.'

'Are you okay to go back to the wards? I'll make your excuses if you need time out.'

'I'm fine,' Zoe said, and managed a bright smile. 'Just a bit…'

'Discombobulated,' Callie said. 'Gutted about Liam's death, like we all are—but with a few layers of emotional confusion on top. Sam, let the lady go. Give her some space.'

'Thank you,' Zoe said, with real gratitude, and gave Sam a quick, hard hug because what he was about to do was one of the hardest things a doctor would ever need to do.

She turned and headed back to her sick kids.

A girl had to do something. Discombobulation didn't begin to describe it.

Alice's wedding was truly lovely. It took place in a tiny chapel in the grounds of one of the Gold Coast's most spectacular beachside hotels. Alice and her brand-new husband were spectacularly in love. The reception was in the hotel grounds overlooking the beach. The weather was balmy, the band was fantastic, and Sam took Zoe in his arms and danced with her, and she thought heaven was right here, right now.

But she felt funny. She'd woken feeling a bit off. She'd shrugged it off as unimportant—there was no way she was missing this wedding—but the more the night wore on the more she felt like she was floating in some sort of fuzzy, hazy dream. It was like she'd been drinking, she thought, trying to keep a handle on what was happening, but she'd had half a glass of champagne early and had switched to mineral water because of the way she was feeling.

Could hormones do this to you?

'Are you okay?' Sam asked at one stage as the number the band was playing came to an end more suddenly than she'd expected and she found herself stumbling. He had to catch her and hold her up.

'I'm fine.' She smiled up at him. 'More than fine.'

'You look more than fine,' he said, and stooped to kiss her. 'You think we should go for a quick walk down to the beach?'

'How about a slow walk down to the beach?' she said, because the way she was feeling there was no way fast was coming into it.

'If you guys are escaping, can I come with you?'

Callie. Of course it was Callie. She was looking

fabulous, in glorious scarlet, in a dress that made Zoe's home-made effort look...well, home-made, but Zoe didn't begrudge her. In the few short weeks Zoe had been at the hospital this woman had become a real friend. She was a solid friend of Sam's as well, so not at all a third wheel.

Even though Zoe suspected Sam might feel she was right now. The way he was holding her...

Too bad, Zoe thought, and realised she was grateful for Callie's presence. She was feeling strange. The way Sam was looking at her was making her feel even more weird. She felt weak at the knees and if Sam took her into his arms in the moonlight and asked her to marry him—as Dean had done on just such a moonlit night—she might even say yes.

'Of course you can come,' Zoe said, before Sam could say a word. 'Are you up for a paddle? I'm so hot.'

'It's not hot,' Sam said.

'It is so,' Callie retorted. 'And if you're not hot now, you go and stand next to Dr Hotshot Cade Coleman. That man is an arrogant bottom-feeder.' Her anger seemed almost palpable.

'You mean he knocked you back?' Sam asked, and Callie glared at Sam and Zoe stared at Sam in shock.

'Sam!'

'Callie's a mate,' Sam said, holding Zoe but smiling at Callie. 'Mates don't take offence.'

'No,' Callie said. 'They don't. And it's true he might have just told me where to get off.' She giggled suddenly, her anger fading. 'Okay, I might have just had one champagne too many, and there might just have been a dare from the theatre girls involved. Whoops,' she said. 'Now I've shocked your country mouse, Sam.'

'I'm not his country mouse,' Zoe said with an attempt at dignity, and wondered just how many champagnes she'd had. She was sure it had only been half a glass. If she hadn't been among friends she'd suspect something had been put in her drink.

'Are you okay?' Callie asked sharply. Of all the questions Zoe hated, that was the worst.

'I'm fine. I want a paddle.'

'I'm not interrupting anything?' Callie asked, and Zoe figured Callie knew very well that she was but she was interrupting anyway. And Zoe was grateful.

'Of course not,' she said, and linked one arm into Callie's and one arm into Sam's and they headed for the beach.

Cade watched them go.

Zoe was almost as new at this hospital as he was, he thought grimly, but she was one of the team already. He, however, was an outsider. He was always an outsider.

Once he'd used women as an escape from himself, but that had been one woman and one baby ago. No more.

And tonight…Callie Richards had come on to him. First she'd insulted him, telling him within days of his arrival at Gold Coast City to steer clear of Zoe Payne. Now, tonight, she'd apologised, asked him to dance and had then made it very clear that if he wanted more…

He didn't want more. He was here to do a job, steer clear of gossip and scandal, retrieve a reputation, block out the past and get on with life.

He shouldn't have come tonight.

He stared after the group of three, Zoe in the middle with Callie and Sam on either side of her, weaving down to the beach, and he suddenly felt an almost overwhelming surge of longing for…something.

The ability to be just a friend?

It wasn't going to happen. Not back in the States. Not here.

He watched them disappear into the darkness and he headed off to find the bride's parents and make his excuses. There was an emergency back at the hospital—he was sure of it.

He wanted an emergency right now.

The water felt delicious on Zoe's toes. She kicked off her sandals, lifted her long skirt to knee length and let the waves wash over and over.

Cool was good. Cool was glorious.

If only the fuzz would disappear.

Callie and Sam were talking behind her, talking to her, but she wasn't sure what they were saying. The night was getting blurrier and blurrier.

'It's time for the speeches,' Sam decreed at last, stepping in between waves to tug her out. He and Callie had left their shoes on and she couldn't figure it out. It was so hot. 'Come on back, love.' Then, as she didn't move fast enough and there was a wave coming he wanted to avoid, he tugged her and she staggered and would have fallen.

She didn't. He swept her into his arms and up to dry sand while she tried to get her bearings.

'I'm okay,' she muttered, before he even asked, but even as she said it, she knew she wasn't.

'Zoe?' It was Callie, reacting to the strange way her words had come out, maybe reacting to Sam's snapped concern. Sam was holding her in his arms.

Callie reached for her hand and winced. 'Sam, she's burning.'

'I'm fine,' she said, but the night was spinning. 'I'm really, really fine.'

'You're ill,' Sam snapped. 'Zoe, what the…? Why didn't you tell us?'

'I'm fine,' she repeated, like a stubborn mantra. How could she not be fine? Sam was holding her. She was in Sam's arms and the night was drifting away— and she wasn't fine at all.

CHAPTER EIGHT

SHE WAS SUFFERING from influenza, courtesy of one bout of mouth-to-mouth resuscitation on a guy who had been suffering from flu before he'd had his heart attack.

Infection was an occupational hazard for medics. It was an occupational hazard for Zoe now that she was a healthy member of the workforce.

But she wasn't healthy now. She spent twenty-four hours in bed in her apartment. Sam and Callie and nearly every other medic Zoe worked with popped in and out, and Bonnie slept on the end of her bed. Zoe felt not quite as ghastly when Bonnie was with her, but she still felt ghastly and bed rest didn't work.

After twenty-four hours, Sam listened to her breathing and demanded chest X-rays. Pneumonia. She then found herself in the third-floor general medical ward. That wasn't very different because the same faces were around her and the same dog was on the end of her bed, but there were intravenous drips and injections and fuss.

She hated fuss.

'Don't tell my parents.' She must have said it a dozen times to Sam and finally he made a poster-sized sign and hung it in the place reserved over her bed for

the 'Nil by mouth' sign used for surgical patients—
only Zoe's sign said: 'Don't Tell Mum and Dad.'

It was a joke, but she couldn't bear it if her parents
knew—for Sam was fussing enough for both of them.

'Why didn't you tell me you felt foul?'

'I don't tell people,' she retorted. 'I don't want fuss.
I just want to be normal.'

'It's normal to tell people you're ill.'

'It's not normal to be ill. Sam, leave it. This is not
a big deal.'

'This is a big deal,' he said stubbornly. 'I should
never have let you—'

'What? Breathe for the guy?' Three days on, she
was recovered enough to argue. She'd had it out with
herself. She'd known the guy had had flu. She'd had
the choice—to wait for a mask and risk him dying, or
breathe when he'd needed breath.

What else could she have done? Cardiac compres-
sions while Sam breathed? That made no sense, because Sam was so much stronger than she was.

'I could have done both,' Sam said, for what must
be the tenth time, and she was fed up.

To tell the truth, she was fed up with more than
Sam's self-blame. She didn't like being back in hospital as a patient—she didn't like it one bit, and she
didn't like the way Sam was treating her. It was flu,
for heaven's sake, not plague.

'We need to put you on the surgical roster when
you're recovered,' Sam said. 'You need to stay out of
medical wards. You don't need to be exposed to any
more viruses.'

'I'm a nurse,' she said. 'Exposure to viruses is part
of my job.'

'You could have died.'

'And so could you if you'd caught pneumonia.'

'I wouldn't.'

'You know very well you could,' she snapped. 'I caught flu and it turned to pneumonia. I've been unlucky. And if you think that this has anything to do with me having a renal transplant—and I know that's what you're thinking, Sam Webster, you have it written all over your face—you can think again. Poor frail little Zoe. I've been there, Sam, and I'm never going there again.'

'I understand that,' he said carefully, 'but you need to be careful.'

'There's care and there's stupid. My mum and dad refused to let me use public transport so I couldn't visit my friends. The mango thing was only part of the stupid restrictions they placed on my life. And Dean...Dean even started carrying antibiotic wipes and recleaning my cutlery at restaurants before I ate. When I told him to stop, he did it by stealth. The last straw was when he rang them and asked them to do it before I got there. The waiter came racing out just before I ate with a *mea culpa* because he'd forgotten. If Dean knew how close he came to wearing my soup...'

He smiled but it was a worried smile. 'I understand how worried he must have been.'

'Do you?' she said dangerously. 'You're justifying bug-kill wipes?'

'No,' he said. 'But I can see why he was worried.'

'I want to go to Nepal,' she said, and he looked at her like she'd announced she was heading for a Mars landing.

'Sorry?'

'Nepal,' she said, watching his face for his reaction and not liking what she was seeing. 'I told you—it's on my list. You can walk all the way to the Anna-purna base camp without needing specialist training. Not now,' she said as she saw his face. 'I may need a couple of years to save, but I will get there.'

'Good for you.'

'There's a nice patronising statement. That's what Mum used to say when I was sick and I'd say as soon as I feel better I'm taking the train to Melbourne to see the new Kylie show. Good for you, she'd say, and then when I was feeling better she'd give me the lat-est Kylie DVD and organise three nice girls to come over and watch it with me. Only not a fourth girl who was my best friend because Robin kept getting colds and Mum wouldn't let her near. Robin got so fed up that we stopped being friends.'

'I'm sorry.'

'I don't want you to be sorry.' It was practically a yell and the sound of her own voice brought her up short.

What was she doing? What was she saying? She was risking everything. But she felt like she was on a runaway train. The doubts had built to the point where she had to have this out with him, and there seemed to be no going back.

'You do think I got this flu because I had a renal transplant,' she said, feeling ill as she said it. 'You don't want me to work with kids who might be infec-tious. What sort of nurse does that make me?'

'It doesn't make you any sort of a nurse,' he said, and raked his hand through his hair. 'Zoe, I know it's unreasonable but how can I stop worrying?'

'You can just…stop.'

'Worrying's about caring. I didn't want to care but I don't seem to have a choice.'

'You don't have to.'

'Like that's possible.' Once again those long, strong fingers raked his hair and she could see his distress. 'Zoe, I lost Emily because I didn't care enough. I should have walked into the surf, picked her up bodily and dragged her out of there. She was being unbelievably stupid. She was crazy that night and I was angry and turned away and made the decision not to care.'

'But you did care,' she said quietly. 'You cared and you cared, but it was Emily's life, Emily's decision, and she had the right to do what she did. Like I have the right to nurse a kid with a cold. Only I'm not stupid, Sam. I know the added risks I have because of my transplant and catching flu isn't one of them.'

'So flu turns into pneumonia...'

'Pneumonia is a known complication for healthy people, too.'

'You collapsed.'

'So I made a mistake. I suspected I was ill,' she admitted. 'I wanted to go to the wedding. I wanted to dance with you.'

'Would you have pushed so hard if you hadn't had the transplant?' It was a harsh question—an accusation.

She lay back on her pillows and glared. She was still weak. She still wanted to have the occasional weep. What she needed right now was to let him hold her, curl up in his arms, let him nurture her, love her... care for her?

She did not want to be cared for.

'Possibly not,' she conceded at last. 'I've spent half my life not feeling well. My friends and family have spent half my life telling me not to do things and I've spent my life aching to do things regardless. So, yes,

I was feeling foul but there was no way I was missing dancing with you.'

He managed a smile at that, and then he touched her cheek, a feather-light touch that did crazy things to her insides. He'd come to see her between visiting his own patients. He looked gorgeous. He smiled at her and she thought he was melt material and she so wanted to melt.

'You know, I think I've fallen in love with you, Zoe,' he said softly. 'I never thought I'd say that again—I'd never thought I could. But you're lovely and cute and brave and funny, and Bonnie loves you and I love what you're doing with your life…'

But there was that one word that made her doubts grow even stronger.

Brave.

'You love that I'm being brave?' She shouldn't say it. She'd said enough. Enough, enough, enough. She was risking so much.

But there were ghosts in her past and one of her ghosts was Dean. Dean had gone to primary school with her, he'd been her friend, he'd been her constant companion.

Dean had loved the sick kid.

It had become his identity, Zoe realised. He'd been boyfriend to the sick kid. He'd loved caring for her, he'd loved it when she'd been in hospital and he could spend hours choosing movies for them to watch, hours worrying about her, fielding her friends, telling them to limit their time with her.

Dean the protector… She'd loved him back, she'd thought, though she'd had to push back the occasional feelings that he was cloying; that he was a barrier to the outside world rather than a conduit. It had only been after the final transplant that she'd realised it was Invalid Zoe who Dean loved. Healthy Zoe wasn't an option.

And here was another guy telling her he loved her—because she was brave.

'I'm not brave,' she muttered. 'I'm normal.'

'You're not normal. You're Zoe.'

'I am normal,' she said, and suddenly she was yelling, which was really inappropriate because she was in a hospital ward and there were people going past in the corridor and the door was open, but all of a sudden she didn't care. 'I'm completely normal. I'm cured. I'm one hundred per cent normal and if you want to fall in love then you fall in love with the normal Zoe and you stop caring!'

'And let you plunge into the surf like Emily did?'

'No. Not like Emily. How can you compare us?' And then she thought about it. 'Or maybe yes. Maybe, yes, like Emily. I'm an adult. I should be able to make my own decisions, stupid or not.'

'You don't think the person who donated your kidney deserves better?'

She stilled at that. Suddenly it seemed the whole world stilled.

That was such a question…

It was a question she asked herself almost every day. She had the answer—sort of. But how to say it to Sam?

'I'm sorry,' he said, before she could find a reply. He was sorry, too. She saw the flash of regret in his eyes, the wish that he could take the question back, but it was out there in the open, demanding an answer.

He deserved an answer, she thought, as Dean had deserved an answer. She'd tried so hard to explain it to him and he hadn't got it. She'd left him hurt, and even her mum's recent phone call to tell her that he was now going out with Monica, who'd come off her motorbike and broken her leg, hadn't alleviated the knowledge that he'd been there for her and in the end she'd had to hurt him to set herself free.

And now she was looking at another man—and the feeling in her stomach was sick and cold.

'*You don't think the person who donated your kidney deserves better?*'

Dean had flung that at her, too, after the transplant when she'd wanted to go dancing. Slightly differently but in the same form.

'*Someone died for you, Zoe. You have a duty to take care of yourself.*'

Put the anger away, she told herself fiercely. Just say it. Say what needs to be said.

'If the boy who died—or his parents who made the decision to donate his organs—had wanted his kidney to be kept in perpetuity, they'd have donated it to the museum,' she managed, trying desperately to keep a lid on emotions that were threatening to overwhelm her. 'They'd have put it in formaldehyde and kept it safe.

'Instead, they elected to use it to let me live. Live, Sam, not wrap myself in cotton wool. I don't want to sit in a jar of formaldehyde for the rest of my life. I want to do every single thing that normal people do. There are things I need to be careful of—I know that. I'm following every single one of my doctor's orders but the last thing he said to me before I left Adelaide was to get out there and have fun. Live life to the full, he said, and that's exactly what I'm doing, except I know my limitations, which is why I'm saying now that I'm recovering from pneumonia and I'm tired and I need to go to sleep. So if you could leave, please…'

'You want me to leave?' He sounded incredulous.

'Yes.'

'Zoe…'

'Sam, I can't do this,' she said miserably. 'I will not be smothered with care. I walked away from Adelaide because I wanted to be free. You're the most gorgeous guy I've ever met—and, okay, I'll admit it, I'm as near to falling in love with you as makes no difference. I also happen to be besotted with your dog, but I won't commit to being smothered. I made the decision that I want to be free and that decision still stands. Back off, Sam, and leave me be.'

'You really mean that?'

'Yes.'

He stood and stared down at her, his face tight and strained. For a long moment there was nothing but silence—a silence that held all the hopes of what might have been but also the knowledge of what had to happen.

Sam was a man who couldn't keep fear at bay, she thought bleakly. He was a man who'd loved once and lost. He was a man who, if he let himself care at all, couldn't help caring too much.

She was a woman who'd had enough of care.

'You'd throw away what we have,' he said at last, and he couldn't disguise his anger, 'because I care.'

'If I must.'

'That's crazy.'

'So I'm crazy, but it's taken me all my life to get this crazy and I'm not going back now.' She took a deep breath, fighting for control. Fighting to get this right.

One part of her was sure she was right. The other was screaming that she was nuts.

But she needed to ignore the part of her that was screaming in anguished protest, the part that was looking at Sam's confusion and wanting to say it didn't matter, she'd love him care and all. For she was not going back to being the Zoe who'd been cared for until she'd felt suffocated.

Why had she come all this way if she was going to sink back into that same sweet trap now? She would not.

So say it and get it over with, she thought, and say it fast, before the anger and confusion she saw on his face broke her resolve.

'Sam, you're awesome,' she said. 'But I don't want this.'

'Because I care.'

'I know it's dumb but yes. There it is. I'm sorry, but enough.'

'Fine,' he said, and his face was rigid with tension—anger? 'Maybe you're right and this is the sensible option. I'm not rational when it comes to relationships any more. I can't do it without fear so it's best if I stand back. I'll wish you luck with your trek in Nepal. I'll expect emails at every summit.'

And he stepped away and it almost killed her. He was back to being consultant cardiologist and colleague. He was backing to the door, backing away to return to his patients, backing out of her life.

But that was what she wanted—right?

No! But it was too late to back down now.

'You're wise for the two of us,' he said, and his voice had changed. The shield had come up again, she thought. He was under control. 'There's no surfing for you this Sunday—even you need to admit you need time to get over this—but as of next Sunday we'll start again. But that's it, Zoe. Lessons and nothing else. You're right—it's the wisest call for both of us.'

'Are you out of your mind?'

Callie was sitting on the end of Zoe's bed—actually, she was practically bouncing with incredulous indignation. 'You have the sexiest doctor in this hospital making a beeline for your bed and you tell him you want to go and climb mountains?'

'He's kind,' Zoe said, knowing as an argument it made no sense, and Callie practically gibbered.

'Yes,' she said. Or was that yelled? 'He's kind. He's toe-curlingly lovely and he's one of the best doctors we have and he's kind to his socks.'

'Then why aren't you interested in him yourself?' Zoe asked, momentarily distracted.

'A, because I'm not interested in relationships, I'm only interested in sex,' Callie said bluntly. 'I've had all the intimate relationships I'm ever going to have. But, even if I wasn't jaded, B, Sam has never looked at me that way. He's never looked at any woman that way since Emily died. And, C, Sam's my friend and I'm not messing with that for the world. But kind? Zoe, you have no idea how important that is. To knock back a man because he's kind…'

'I'm done with kindness.'

How bad did that sound? Zoe thought. She sounded like a sulky child who didn't like her chosen-with-love Christmas gift. She was being totally unreasonable. She also knew she could well regret what she was doing for the rest of her life, but still she had to do it.

'You know, getting over a kidney transplant takes

all sorts of courage,' Callie said gently, changing track, and she winced.

'This isn't about a kidney transplant.'

'I think it is.' Callie went on, inexorably. 'Like Sam's worry is more because he lost Emily. You two have ghosts, but if you worked on it, maybe your ghosts could indulge in mutual trauma therapy while the real Sam and the real Zoe went at it like rabbits.'

'Callie!'

'Just saying,' Callie said, and hauled herself off the bed. 'But ghosts are everywhere and they need to be catered for. I have a few of my own that mess with my life. Meanwhile, I need to go—I have patients to see. Uncomplicated kids with their ghosts just forming. But think about it, Zoe. Are you going to let ghosts stand in the way of grabbing Sam and holding on?'

'I suspect you know very well that ghosts can't be put aside at will,' Zoe said, watching the shadows on her friend's face. 'You don't hold on to anyone. And coming on to Cade like you did…is that your ghosts?'

'Yeah, now we're getting personal,' Callie said, and managed a wry smile. 'I suspect all our ghosts could have a field day together. Mine and yours and Sam's.'

'And Cade's?' This was better, Zoe thought. Talking about other ghosts than hers.

'Cade's?'

'You know he's carrying baggage, and that baggage is striking off yours. The sparks at the wedding—'

'Were the result of champagne and a dare and nothing else,' Callie said soundly. 'Cade Coleman is an arrogant low-life and I want nothing more to do with him. Unlike Sam…'

'They're both just guys,' Zoe said, gloom descending again. 'But you're right, maybe the ghosts are too strong for all of us.'

Callie left and she was alone with her ghosts.

She lay and let them drift.

Her ghosts had made her set rules, she thought. Those rules were important. But had those rules messed with the most important thing that had ever happened to her? Sam?

'I can't help it,' she whispered. 'I can't be smothered. We'd both be unhappy. It's best this way.'

Sure it was. So why did she cover her face with her pillow and close her eyes to try and stop the ghosts from shouting?

'Why the long face? You're better out of it and you know it.'

Sam and Cade had just spent a fraught two hours with a neonate with a heart defect. Rebecca Louise Hayden was six hours old, and for a while it had looked as if she'd get no older. But finally they'd had her stabilised enough for Sam to speak to her distraught parents and tell them that this was a long road, Rebecca had more surgery in front of her, more challenges, but that he and Cade were cautiously optimistic.

Now the two men stood over the incubator in the preemie ward, looked down at the scrap of life that was Rebecca—such a big name for a tiny thread of life—and Cade unexpectedly brought up Sam's love life. Or lack of it.

How the hell did he know that Zoe had ditched him? Sam thought morosely. But, then, how did anyone in this hospital know anything? Osmosis? Someone should write a thesis.

'Yeah, relationships only cause problems,' he

agreed, and turned to look out the ward window. From the third floor you could see the sea. It was glittering in the afternoon sun and he had an almost irresistible urge to walk out of the hospital and go ride a wave.

He couldn't walk away from Rebecca. He couldn't walk away from his work.

He had to walk away from Zoe.

'You're better without them, mate,' Cade said, and Sam glanced at the guy on the other side of the cot. He thought how hard Cade had worked with him to get this tiny baby to the other side of the survival odds and he thought there was stuff in this guy's past as well.

'So you've had three wives, six kids and five mistresses?'

'Not quite,' Cade said, and smiled, only the smile was a bit grim. 'Enough, though.'

'You want to try surfing. It helps.'

'Nothing helps.'

'Sheesh,' Sam said. 'Eight wives?'

He got a grin. He was starting to like this guy. Cade held the rest of the staff at arm's length—he seemed prickly and arrogant—but Sam saw the care that went into Cade's interaction with his little patients and he sensed the arrogance was a shield.

So many shields.

'You still teaching Zoe?' Cade asked.

'Um…yeah.'

'You want me to join your surfing lessons?'

'No,' he said, before his mind could talk sense.

Cade's grin grew wider. 'So you still hold some hope.'

'Not much.'

'You give up and you're dead,' Cade said, and his

gaze went back to tiny Rebecca. 'You fight and fight and fight until you can't fight any longer.'

'And then you come to Australia?'

Cade's smile faded.

'Not your business,' he muttered. 'Okay, here's the deal. You stay out of my private concerns and I'll stay out of yours.'

'I will teach you to surf,' Sam said. 'But not with Zoe.'

'I'll buy myself a board and teach myself to surf.' Cade put a gloved hand through the incubator port and touched the tiny girl's cheek—a feather touch—one large finger against a face that was smaller than his palm. 'Independence…you fight for yourself right from the start. It never stops and the sooner you accept it the better for everyone.'

'Rebecca needed us.'

'So she did,' Cade said. 'And we helped and now we back off.'

Zoe's convalescence lasted more than a week. She had a couple of bad days when she realised she wasn't eligible for sick leave yet due to still being on her probation period at the hospital. She thought she'd not be paid and she'd end up eating home-brand pasta for a month, but come payday her bank account was healthy. It appeared that because she'd caught flu from giving CPR to a Gold Coast City patient her time off was covered by the hospital. The paperwork had been organised by Sam.

He was still in the background. He was still dropping Bonnie off at her apartment every morning, but he wasn't staying. In, out, gone.

She tried not to mind. She and Bonnie recovered

together. They slept. They took gentle walks along the beach. They sat in the morning sun and shared ice cream, and they treated themselves with care.

They'd both rather that Sam was with them. Zoe only had to look at Bonnie when she heard footsteps approaching—how fast her big head swivelled and the way she sort of drooped when it wasn't Sam—to know how much Bonnie loved him, and she tried not to, but she felt exactly the same.

The ghosts were yelling she was crazy, crazy, crazy.

'You're never satisfied,' she told them. 'What do you want me to do? Be cosseted for the rest of my life? Is that what you want?'

They didn't answer. Ghosts made lousy communicators. They were all accusation and nothing else.

Sunday was the hardest. She wasn't fit enough for a surfing lesson; she knew she wasn't, but Sam was going anyway, taking Bonnie with him. He dropped in to pick up Bonnie's flags and trampoline bed.

She watched them go and she felt…desolate.

He surfed and he thought of Zoe.

How could he stop caring?

He couldn't. He just…couldn't. Emily's death had hit him too hard for him to stand back and take risks.

Everyone took risks. He knew that. For him to say Zoe shouldn't work with kids who might be infectious had been over the top. He knew that, too. He should say it to her, but it wouldn't make a difference. It nearly killed him that she'd caught pneumonia and he knew that the next time she was in harm's way he'd react exactly the same.

How to stand back and let the woman he loved take risks?

He'd crowded her, he'd scared her, but it was Zoe's problem as well as his, he thought. He cared too much and she didn't want care.

Catch 22. There was no solution but to surf.

He didn't go far out. He was too aware of Bonnie lying on her trampoline bed, surrounded by Zoe's crazy flags.

The flags made him smile.

Zoe cared.

The perfect wave swept up behind him and he missed it.

He swore and rolled one eighty degrees so he was lying under his board rather than on top of it. He stayed underwater until it was necessary to surface if he was to breathe. He surfaced spluttering, hoping he'd vented enough spleen, but his spleen wasn't vented.

He missed another wave.

'How can I love her and not care?' he demanded of the universe, but the universe didn't answer. In his experience it rarely did.

Impasse. There was no solution at all.

CHAPTER NINE

WORK WAS A welcome relief. It was great to be back on the wards, Zoe thought, even if ward work came with sympathy that the promising affair between Zoe Payne and Sam Webster seemed to have fizzled out.

She met him occasionally on the ward. They greeted each other as warmly as both could manage, aware that every eye was on them, but it was strained and by Wednesday Zoe was starting to wonder if she should request a transfer to one of the adult wards. Somewhere a paediatric cardiologist was unlikely to visit.

But then she wouldn't see him at all—and that hurt.

Everything hurt.

'What's happening with Bonnie?' she asked as he finished examining a little boy who'd been admitted with rheumatic fever, who'd recovered but was showing signs of heart strain.

'She's back on the wards, too,' he told her.

'Back?'

'Her day job while I work is spending time with patients who need her. There's an old lady in the trauma unit. She and her husband were in a car accident three weeks ago and her husband died. Bonnie's asleep on her bed. Hospital rules say basket on the floor even for companion animals but no one's shifting Bonnie.'

'That's lovely,' Zoe whispered. 'Bonnie's awesome.'

'She's not the only lady who's awesome,' Sam said and left, with her staring after him.

How could she not want him to care? Was she out of her mind?

But the memories of the smothering were too strong, too real for her to put them aside. She could cast herself on his chest right now, she thought, and the webs of care would go round her again and she'd wake up feeling strangled. She knew she would.

And yet she felt terrible. Her family may have smothered her during her years of illness but at least they'd been there. They were still there, she told herself, but it didn't help. Why did she feel so gut-wrenchingly, desolately alone?

'Katie Foster's wet her bed,' her colleague Hannah told her, cutting across her chain of bleak thoughts. 'And she's mortified. Strain does bad things to kids. You want to read her a story while I change the sheets?'

'Of course,' Zoe said, and went to read to a morti-fied Katie, but while she did she thought...

Strain did bad things to kids.

Strain was doing bad things to her.

Wednesday night and she was going nuts. After work she walked on the beach near the hospital but it wasn't enough. There were too many tourists, too many peo-ple, not enough space for her thoughts.

On impulse she took her car—it only took three attempts to start—bought fish and chips and headed out to the Seaway to eat them.

It'd be lovely out there. This late midweek there'd only be the odd surfer.

That surfer might be Sam, but she carefully put that thought aside. If it was Sam she could sit in the sand hills and watch from a distance. He didn't have to know she was there.

He wasn't there. She seemed to have the beach to herself, except for a couple of kids far along the beach. She settled on a sand hill and ate her fish and chips and thought how Dean would have told her off for eating fatty food, and she ate a few more chips in his honour. And then she thought of Sam and she defiantly ate a few more.

'I don't want anyone caring,' she said out loud, and it sounded stupid. It was stupid. And bleak.

She wouldn't mind compromising.

But Sam wasn't interested in compromising, she told herself. It was all or nothing. He wouldn't even want her nursing kids who might have a cold. Huh!

Kids.

She glanced along the beach to where the kids were playing, and she thought…hang on. Where were they?

They'd been just there.

Just…just…

She stared a bit longer and saw sand sliding down. Masses of sand.

Dear God.

A car was pulling into the car park just above her. She glanced wildly round and it was Sam, lifting Bonnie out of the passenger seat.

'Sam!' Her scream was so loud it was like it cut the beach. 'Sam…the kids have dug into the cliff again and it looks like it's come down on them.'

Sam was heading to his evening surf but he'd been having trouble looking forward to it. Bonnie's great head was on his knee and the Labrador seemed to pick up his moods—when he was sad, so was she. He had the radio up loud, trying to gear himself up with a corny Elvis song, but Bonnie wasn't fooled. She was heaving sighs as if she was thinking exactly what he was thinking.

Where's Zoe?

He was being dumb. All he had to do was back off in the care department and they could have fun. But…

'Come on, Sam, don't be a wuss, the surf's fine.' They were the last words he'd heard from Emily and they echoed through his head every night of his life.

Don't be a wuss, the surf's fine.

Risk.

He couldn't bear it, he thought savagely. He couldn't bear watching Zoe, knowing that something could happen, knowing she could be snatched away. And to watch her and pretend not to care…it was enough to make a guy go nuts.

He needed to surf. He needed to do anything rather than think of Zoe.

He climbed out of the car, reached in to lift Bonnie down—and a scream came from the beach below.

'Sam… The kids have dug into the cave again and it looks like it's come down on them.'

Zoe!

He put Bonnie back into the Jeep and slammed the door.

He ran.

The council had bulldozed the overhang, making it safe—unless you were a kid who knew there was a cave hidden behind the bulldozed sand and you'd decided to dig back in and find it. And now…it looked like a whole slab of the foreshore had caved in, on top of whoever was inside.

Zoe had started running even as she'd screamed. She reached the collapsed section before Sam, and by the time he got there she was already hurling herself at the sand, scraping great swathes of it away using her looped arms as a scoop.

'They're in there,' she gasped as Sam reached her. 'I saw them. I think it was the same boys we saw…'

'You're sure?'

'They were just here. I was throwing chips for the seagulls and then…and then they weren't here any more.'

'H-help.' It was a faint, muffled cry, really muffled, but it had them pausing, staring at the mound of collapsed cliff, trying to figure where…where…

'Stay absolutely still,' Sam yelled. 'Tug your shirts over your mouths and noses and don't move. Not one muscle. We're coming but it will take time. Do not move!' He was scooping at the sand, using Zoe's method but with ten times more strength. Sand was being shoved aside with a force Zoe hadn't thought possible.

'We need a spade,' Sam threw at her. 'Zoe, stop. We need help, and it's up to you to get it. See the lifesaver station? It's empty and locked apart from weekends. It's up on stilts so you need to swing yourself up. The windows are barred, the whole place is locked, but the base is made of plywood. Kick it in and get spades, and masks and oxygen. Go. You have a phone? Use it while you run. Ask for fire services—they have the heavy moving equipment—but ask for ambulance back-up. The Seaway Spit, south of the car park. Got it? Go?'

He was digging deeper as he clipped orders, deeper, deeper, and Zoe looked at the mass of slippery sand around and above him and gave a sob of fear.

'Go,' he snapped, and she went.

She screamed into the phone for emergency services, and somehow she made herself coherent enough to be understood. 'Two kids buried by cliff collapse at South Seaway Beach. Bring digging equipment, men, medics.'

How far did they have to come? Oh, God... She ran with the image of partly collapsed cliff hanging over Sam's head. Why wasn't she with him?

She was following orders.

The deserted lifeguard tower was a high yellow cube on stilts, with steel grates over the windows. The door was eight feet from the ground. A ladder hung underneath, firmly locked so no one could tug it down.

She wasn't great at breaking locks and she didn't even consider it. Instead, she jumped and clung, monkeylike, to the first strut. She thought, *You can do this, Zoe*, and before her sensible side told her no way, she swung herself harder, up to the next strut, then up and onto the platform so she was somehow balanced on the thin, unwelcoming doorstep.

Inside there'd be spades and masks and oxygen. Sam had said there would be. There had to be. Sand collapse must be something these guys would be equipped for.

The door was padlocked. The grilles were immovable. Kick in the plywood, Sam had said, so that's exactly what she did, and she kicked harder than she'd ever kicked in her life. She heard—and felt—her toe give an ominous crack but she was through. The plywood splintered and she could haul pieces clear, enough to wiggle inside to find what she wanted.

God bless lifesavers. There seemed a place for everything and everything in its place. It took her a whole twenty seconds to grab what she needed from the carefully labelled cupboards.

She shoved everything out through the hole and let it fall—she could hardly climb with shovels and oxygen cylinders and masks. She worried fleetingly about tossing oxygen but she hardly had a choice. Equipment hit the sand and she hit the sand seconds after it.

Her toe told her it was broken. She told it not to whinge. She grabbed her booty into one huge armful and ran again.

All the while thinking Sam…

And two kids. She *was* thinking two kids, it was just that Sam was there, too, and this was Sam and she was feeling…

Sick, empty, terrified.

So she ran and searched the beach in front of her—and he was gone.

Gone?

There was only a swathe of freshly collapsed sand.

The last of the cliff above had come down.

Oh, God…

But as she neared the collapse…a hand surfaced above the sand, and then…then a head, coated by a shirt. He hauled the shirt away and coughed and shoved sand from his face.

Sam! It was all she could do not to scream. He was

waving to her to hurry and she couldn't run any further, her lungs were about to explode.

'Masks?' he yelled, before she reached him. 'Oxygen?'

She was there, staring hopelessly at what was before her. There was so much sand above Sam. It could still slip.

'They're in here and they're alive,' he snapped, as she reached the foot of the mound. 'There's a scooped-out spot that's letting them breathe but I can't haul them out without bringing the whole mass down. Hand me the masks and canister.'

'Sam, come out.'

'Start digging from the edge and don't put any pressure on the top,' he said abruptly, and reached out, sand coated, buried to his shoulders, grabbing what he needed. 'Is help coming?'

'I… Yes.'

'We need manpower and care and luck. Dig from the left, Zoe, and make them take care. It's up to you to make sure they don't stuff it.'

He shoved a mask across his mouth, swiped his eyes, checked the oxygen canister—and then, unbelievably, he ducked down again. The sand seemed to ooze over his head and he disappeared from sight.

'Sam!'

'Dig,' came the muffled response, and then nothing.

She dug from the side like a woman possessed, but the amount of sand was massive. She'd made no headway at all before the emergency services arrived—fire, police, ambulance. She gave them stark facts, she was put aside and the big guns went to work.

It wasn't brute force—it couldn't be. They still had to use care but there were men here much better with spades than she was. Even though they could no longer hear anyone, the assumption was that there was a cave somewhere inside that mass of sand, that three people were alive in that cave, and there was no way they were going to bring the whole thing down. A guy arrived from the council, an engineer with a truckload of shoring timber. That stopped the sand slipping back down where they'd dug.

'They'll be using every ounce of energy to breathe,' the fire chief told her. 'If they have masks and oxygen and they're not crushed, they have a chance. If they have sense—and if Dr Webster's with them he'll give them sense—they'll lie stock-still and not touch their masks. To shift a mask to yell could mean catastrophe. So don't give up hope, girl. We'll reach them but we need to do it with care.'

She had to leave them to it. It was the hardest thing she'd ever done but there was only room for about six men to dig and they wanted the strongest, the burliest, and Zoe didn't fit the job description.

She backed off. She went and let Bonnie out of the car then sat on the sand and hugged Bonnie and watched until her eyes ached.

Bonnie stared, too. It was as if she knew.

People were coming from everywhere now as the news spread. Callie came rushing down from the car park, still in her white coat with her stethoscope swinging. She stopped short when she saw Zoe. She stared at the mass of caved-in sand and she, too, slumped to the sand and hugged Bonnie.

Zoe hardly noticed. She had eyes only for the diggers.

The cops were putting up a line of yellow plastic tape, keeping onlookers out. The search was getting methodical.

The boys' parents arrived, distraught and hysterical. The cops had to restrain them from throwing themselves at the cliff.

Oh, God, how long had it been? Twenty minutes? More?

'They must have gone right into the cliff,' the fire chief said grimly. He was overseeing operations right by where Zoe knelt with Bonnie and Callie. By rights he should ask them to go to the other side of the tape but they weren't moving and he wasn't asking. 'We're reaching the end of the soft sand—they must have burrowed right in behind. That's good but it also makes our job harder. There's so much stuff that can still come down.'

Zoe gave a sob of fear and clung harder to Bonnie. Bonnie shoved her big head into her armpit and seemed to hug back.

Callie hugged them both.

Waiting. It was the hardest, hardest thing.

She thought suddenly of her parents, of all those years in waiting rooms, waiting for the news of their daughter's health.

Worrying. Frantic with fear.

She'd known at a superficial level but not like this. Dear God, to love someone and have to wait…

She loved him. She loved Sam. She loved him with every ounce of energy she had within her.

He'd said he was falling in love with her.

She'd pushed him away because he cared.

She cared so much now she was going crazy. She

was dying inside, every minute killing her as the spades dug in, as the timbers were put up so they could dig in a few more inches, as the moments ticked by…

And then…

A shout.

'They're in here. All still. More timbers…'

The crowd behind the tape hushed. The whole world hushed. No one breathed.

More timbers went sliding in. The fire chief barked instructions. There was a change of the order at the site, someone ducked low into the timber-lined chasm, and there was more silence.

And then…

One of the diggers, hard hatted and masked, backed out, tugging…

A boy…

There was a sob of fear from behind her, a woman lurched forward and was restrained…

Arms lifted the boy, sand-coated, masked. Someone tugged the mask free and the child looked around and saw his mother…

'M-Mum.'

There was a collective gasp as the paramedics moved in to do their job. Callie rose to help but Zoe was no longer watching. Her attention was back with the diggers.

Please…

Another shout. Another child was pulled free. They were using shoring timbers to hold him flat and someone yelled for Callie.

Spinal injuries?

But he, too, quavered a whisper as his parents reached him.

Please…

And then, emerging behind the board...looking like the abominable sandman, coated from head to foot, letting men pull him, blinking in the light, wiping his face, accepting a towel and brushing sand away, hauling the mask off and shaking his head as paramedics moved in...

Sam.

She couldn't move. She could only stare. Sam.

Alive.

He was searching the crowd. Men were gripping his shoulders, one of the paramedics was offering mask and oxygen, but he was searching...

He found her.

His gaze met hers.

And right there, right then Bonnie realised that this sand-coated apparition was the guy she loved with all her heart. Unequivocally. No conditions. The big Labrador bounded forward with as much bounce as her splinted leg allowed, and Sam was covered in Labrador, he had his dog in his arms but he was striding forward as he hugged, and somehow she was standing and moving as well.

And then he reached her. 'D-down,' Sam said in a voice that was none too steady. 'Sit.'

And Bonnie subsided and sat and Sam Webster looked at Zoe Payne and there was something in that look that was a marriage vow all by itself.

'You got help,' he said, and she blinked back tears and reached for his hands and held and held and held.

'You got out.'

'I had to get out for you.'

'I don't suppose it's any use for me to say never, ever, ever do anything so terrifying ever in your life again,' she whispered. 'Sam, I thought you were going to die.'

'I thought I might,' he said. They were almost formal. They were standing holding hands while the rest of the world watched, while people grinned their approval, while the world came to terms with this rescue and while Zoe and Sam came to terms with something new. With the rest of their lives.

'I couldn't bear it,' she whispered. 'To lose you.'

'I guess we'll have to bear it one day,' he said. 'But not today. I'm giving us sixty years.'

'Not if you keep taking risks like today.'

'I couldn't not,' he said soberly, looking back at the collapsed sand. 'I couldn't not go in there. Like you can't stop nursing kids with sniffles. Or climbing mountains. It's who we are.'

'But I love you, Sam,' she said, and it was a vow. 'If you ever scare me like that again I'll…'

'You'll?'

'I'll love you more,' she whispered, and at last she fell forward and he tugged her into his arms. He was a mass of sand, it felt like hugging a crumbed rissole, but he was her Sam, he was here, he was alive, and he was…

Sam.

'I'll let you worry,' she whispered.

'That's big of you,' he said into her hair.

'But I need to worry back.'

'Granted,' he said, and tugged back and tilted her chin so he could look into her eyes. 'Zoe, I might get paranoid…'

'And I'll tell you you're paranoid. I might get dumb and try to climb mountains too big for me.'

'Then I'll tell you you're dumb.'

'I foresee fights.'

'I like a decent fight. Will you let me win?'

'Half the time,' she said. 'We'll put a chart on the refrigerator. Fifty per cent me, fifty per cent you. Sam...'

'Mmm?'

'When Dean cared...he loved me because he could care. He loved me because he loved worrying. It took me years to figure it out and it scared me.'

'And when Emily took risks she took them because she loved taking risks,' Sam said, just as gravely. 'I can't tell you how much that scared me. You reckon, though, if we know what we're fighting, we can work through it?'

'We can try,' she said shakily.

'Zoe?'

'Mmm?'

'I think that's enough negotiation for one afternoon,' he said, and suddenly there was no hint of shakiness in his voice. This was Dr Sam Webster who'd just saved two lives. This was Dr Sam Webster who was standing in the late afternoon sun holding the woman he loved. This was Dr Sam Webster about to kiss the woman he loved with all his heart.

There was no more prevarication. The time was right to kiss his Zoe—and he did.

Callie was helping to load the two kids into the ambulance when Cade arrived. Word must have gone around the hospital like wildfire—every off-duty medic from Gold Coast City seemed to be on the beach now. These kids couldn't possibly get better attention.

Cade saw Callie and headed straight for her.

'Status?' he said in the clipped, unemotional tone of an emergency physician working out triage.

'No deaths,' Callie said, responding to his tone and trying to keep her voice unemotional. 'Two teenagers, one with a smashed shoulder, the other with suspected fractured hip, possible ribs, query spine, but there's movement so we're not looking at paraplegia.'

'And Sam?'

Sam was Cade's colleague, Callie thought. They'd only worked together for a few weeks but Callie knew there was already respect and friendship between the two men.

'He managed to get himself through falling sand into the cave they were buried in,' she said. 'He took in masks and oxygen and kept them alive until help arrived.'

'He's okay?'

She gestured down to the beach where one man and one woman were totally entwined, kissing as if there was no tomorrow, even though there was a crowd around them and one chocolate-coloured Labrador was nudging between them with increasing impatience.

'What do you think?'

Cade stared down the beach for a long moment, and his mouth twisted into a wry grimace.

'Love conquers all,' he said, and he couldn't disguise the sarcasm.

'So it seems,' Callie said steadily.

'You're going to advise her to cut and run?'

'I'm not advising anyone,' Callie said. 'I know nothing and understand less. I love it that they're happy. I hope it lasts.'

'Me, too,' Cade said unexpectedly. 'Other people can be happy. Just not us, right?'

'You've got it in one,' she said, and turned back to help load two battered kids into the ambulance.

Sunday.

It was surfing lesson number twenty-nine and she did it.

She hit the green room.

The green room was a special, magic place, known only to surfers who've been surfing for years. Zoe wasn't ready. The great, curling wave came from nowhere. If Sam had had time he'd have yelled to Zoe to let it go, it was too big, she wasn't expert enough.

She caught it with ease.

He'd been lying on his board two hundred yards away. The great wave curled towards him.

He could watch over it and wait with fear until Zoe came out the other end—*if* Zoe came out the other end—or he could catch it himself.

The board lifted him and he pushed forward and felt the magic force as wave and board came together.

It curled high, high, higher…and over.

He was totally enclosed, a ring of green water, a tunnel pushing him forward. Sunlight glinting through the green walls. Force was all around him. Breathtaking beauty.

Somewhere in the same wave was Zoe.

He could hold his breath in terror or ride his wave, and somehow there was no room for terror.

The green room enclosed him in its magic and somehow he knew that the magic was closing around Zoe as well.

His surfing girl. His Zoe.

The wave was an endless curve, a once-in-a-lifetime ride, curling more and more for almost the full length of the beach. He rode its length until it fell away as the beach became shallow, as the green room became a simple breaking wave washing to the shore. He emerged to sunlight and to a whoop of pure joy from twenty yards away.

He turned and she was there, laughing, crying, joyous, his beautiful surfer girl. His Zoe.

He'd meant to wait. He'd had it planned, a three-week holiday to Nepal, a trek to the base of Annapurna Two, a candlelit dinner organised by sherpas, a ring, a question.

Instead, he paddled the few feet between them, he tugged her from the board, he lifted her into his arms and he kissed her so deeply he knew that no time would be more perfect.

No woman would be more perfect.

Somehow he unfastened their leg ropes, letting the tide carry their boards to the shore. She smiled and smiled, as if she knew what was coming, as if she, too, knew the perfection of this moment.

He put her down, he sank to one knee—and a wave knocked him sideways.

He surfaced spluttering, to find her choked with laughter and sinking to her knees to join him.

'You drown, we drown together,' she told him.

'Does that mean you'll marry me?''

There was a long, long silence while four more waves washed over them, while more curling waves broke and ran for shore, while the world settled on its axis to what was right, what was perfect, what was now.

'Why, yes,' Zoe whispered at last as he drew her close. 'Why, yes, Sam Webster, I believe it does.'

He whooped with joy. He kissed her long and deep and with all the love in his heart.

And then one brown Labrador bounded into the water to join them, a kiss became a sandwich hug and Sam Webster and Zoe Payne became a family.

* * * * *

GOLD COAST ANGELS:
TWO TINY HEARTBEATS
by Fiona McArthur,
the next story in this fabulous series,
is also available this month.

Mills & Boon® Hardback

October 2013

ROMANCE

The Greek's Marriage Bargain	Sharon Kendrick
An Enticing Debt to Pay	Annie West
The Playboy of Puerto Banús	Carol Marinelli
Marriage Made of Secrets	Maya Blake
Never Underestimate a Caffarelli	Melanie Milburne
The Divorce Party	Jennifer Hayward
A Hint of Scandal	Tara Pammi
A Façade to Shatter	Lynn Raye Harris
Whose Bed Is It Anyway?	Natalie Anderson
Last Groom Standing	Kimberly Lang
Single Dad's Christmas Miracle	Susan Meier
Snowbound with the Soldier	Jennifer Faye
The Redemption of Rico D'Angelo	Michelle Douglas
The Christmas Baby Surprise	Shirley Jump
Backstage with Her Ex	Louisa George
Blame It on the Champagne	Nina Harrington
Christmas Magic in Heatherdale	Abigail Gordon
The Motherhood Mix-Up	Jennifer Taylor

MEDICAL

Gold Coast Angels: A Doctor's Redemption	Marion Lennox
Gold Coast Angels: Two Tiny Heartbeats	Fiona McArthur
The Secret Between Them	Lucy Clark
Craving Her Rough Diamond Doc	Amalie Berlin

0913 GEN STD HB

Mills & Boon® Large Print
October 2013

ROMANCE

The Sheikh's Prize	Lynne Graham
Forgiven but not Forgotten?	Abby Green
His Final Bargain	Melanie Milburne
A Throne for the Taking	Kate Walker
Diamond in the Desert	Susan Stephens
A Greek Escape	Elizabeth Power
Princess in the Iron Mask	Victoria Parker
The Man Behind the Pinstripes	Melissa McClone
Falling for the Rebel Falcon	Lucy Gordon
Too Close for Comfort	Heidi Rice
The First Crush Is the Deepest	Nina Harrington

HISTORICAL

Reforming the Viscount	Annie Burrows
A Reputation for Notoriety	Diane Gaston
The Substitute Countess	Lyn Stone
The Sword Dancer	Jeannie Lin
His Lady of Castlemora	Joanna Fulford

MEDICAL

NYC Angels: Unmasking Dr Serious	Laura Iding
NYC Angels: The Wallflower's Secret	Susan Carlisle
Cinderella of Harley Street	Anne Fraser
You, Me and a Family	Sue MacKay
Their Most Forbidden Fling	Melanie Milburne
The Last Doctor She Should Ever Date	Louisa George

Mills & Boon® Hardback

November 2013

ROMANCE

MEDICAL

ROMANCE

His Most Exquisite Conquest	Emma Darcy
One Night Heir	Lucy Monroe
His Brand of Passion	Kate Hewitt
The Return of Her Past	Lindsay Armstrong
The Couple who Fooled the World	Maisey Yates
Proof of Their Sin	Dani Collins
In Petrakis's Power	Maggie Cox
A Cowboy To Come Home To	Donna Alward
How to Melt a Frozen Heart	Cara Colter
The Cattleman's Ready-Made Family	Michelle Douglas
What the Paparazzi Didn't See	Nicola Marsh

HISTORICAL

Mistress to the Marquis	Margaret McPhee
A Lady Risks All	Bronwyn Scott
Her Highland Protector	Ann Lethbridge
Lady Isobel's Champion	Carol Townend
No Role for a Gentleman	Gail Whitiker

MEDICAL

NYC Angels: Flirting with Danger	Tina Beckett
NYC Angels: Tempting Nurse Scarlet	Wendy S. Marcus
One Life Changing Moment	Lucy Clark
P.S. You're a Daddy!	Dianne Drake
Return of the Rebel Doctor	Joanna Neil
One Baby Step at a Time	Meredith Webber